John Collins

Reminiscences of Isaac and Rachel Budd Collins

with an account of some of their descendants, together with a genealogy of the Collins family, and also a history of a reunion held at Philadelphia, May 9, 1892

John Collins

Reminiscences of Isaac and Rachel Budd Collins
with an account of some of their descendants, together with a genealogy of the Collins family, and also a history of a reunion held at Philadelphia, May 9, 1892

ISBN/EAN: 9783337734145

Printed in Europe, USA, Canada, Australia, Japan

Cover: Foto ©Raphael Reischuk / pixelio.de

More available books at **www.hansebooks.com**

REMINISCENCES

OF

ISAAC AND RACHEL (BUDD) COLLINS.

WITH AN ACCOUNT OF

SOME OF THEIR DESCENDANTS,

TOGETHER WITH

A GENEALOGY OF THE COLLINS FAMILY,

AND ALSO

A HISTORY OF A REUNION HELD AT PHILADELPHIA,
MAY 9, 1892.

PREFACE.

At a reunion of the descendants of Isaac and Rachel Collins, held May 9, 1892, a committee was appointed to prepare a history of the Collins family, and to publish with this such reminiscences of Isaac and Rachel Collins and other members of the family as might prove interesting. While the information in some particulars may be considered brief, it is believed that no important facts have been omitted, and what is presented will be of value to all who are directly or remotely connected with the Collins ancestry.

John Collins,
Isaac Collins,
Thomas G. Morton, M.D.,
Morris Earle.

May 16, 1893.

INTRODUCTION.

The following brief history of Isaac and Rachel Collins has been compiled from family records, letters, and traditions. Unfortunately, the family records which belonged to Isaac Collins were destroyed by fire at Trenton, New Jersey, and his attempt to obtain information of his family subsequently through advertisements inserted in the Bristol (England) newspapers does not appear to have been successful.

The committee are well aware of the incompleteness of the work now presented, but all has been accomplished which seemed possible with the limited amount of material and the inability of the committee to obtain assistance from an inspection of some family records.

Brief memoirs of other members of the family will be found in the appendix, and likewise short biographical sketches of several who, being connected by marriage with the Collins family, have, from their religious or scientific attainments, worthily earned the right of mention.

The object of the committee has been, however,

to present the life, character, and virtues of Isaac Collins and his beloved wife in such a form as can be made available for future reference.

Recent efforts made for a similar purpose in this country and abroad to secure additional information of the Collins ancestry have met with but little success.

It is believed, however, that the accompanying history of Isaac and Rachel Collins, brief as it is, will prove interesting to the various members of the family.

FIRST RESIDENCE OF ISAAC COLLINS.

REMINISCENCES

OF

ISAAC AND RACHEL (BUDD) COLLINS.

CHARLES COLLINS, father of Isaac Collins, came to America from Bristol, England, about the year 1734, when he was nineteen years of age. He married Sarah Hammond, and had two children,—Elizabeth and Isaac. After her death he married Elizabeth Neal, by whom he had two children,—Sarah and William. Elizabeth never married and William died when young. Of Sarah but little is known. The parents of Isaac Collins, both of whom belonged to the Society of Friends, died during his childhood, and little is known of his family, from the fact stated in one of his letters, that the family records were destroyed by fire.

A letter written by Isaac Collins to William Dillwyn, dated Fourth month 24, 1774, gives some interesting facts.

"After my father's decease his widow married again and removed into a remote part of the country from where I dwelt, and I have not seen her for fourteen years, nor since I have had a desire for correspondence with some of my uncles or cousins, and by that means

I have been prevented from getting a good traditional knowledge.

"I cannot call all my uncles by name, nor am I certain of the number, but, according to the best of my remembrance, my father's eldest brother's name was John Collins, who, after the death of his father, was entrusted with the care of his brethren, and by whom my father was put out an apprentice to a wine-cooper in Bristol, England. I think I have been told that I had an uncle named Robert and another William, and after the last mentioned my brother William had his name. My father had a brother who followed the sea—was captain or commander of a vessel which had sailed to New York, and for aught I know was in that trade. He had a liberal education in the Episcopal Church. He has been dead about twenty-one years.

"As I have but few relations by my mother's side, and as I conceive there is great pleasure in having an acquaintance with both, I am thus solicitous, which I hope will be sufficient apology for my requesting thee to take some pains in this matter; but if thou canst get no Tidings from personal inquiry, be pleased to publish the enclosed Advertisement in the Bristol News Paper or such others as will best effect the purpose."

Isaac Collins was born on the 16th of Second month, 1746, near the Brandywine Creek, about two miles from Centre Meeting-House, in New Castle County, Delaware. The quaint old building still stands there by the road-side, no longer used for a place of religious worship. The graveyard in the rear shows many grass-grown mounds, with rude head-stones sunk almost out of sight or overgrown with yearly verdure. A careful search did not result in finding the name of Collins on any of the tablets. An examination of such of the old records of the meeting as have been saved, disclosed nothing relating to the membership, the marriage, or the death of Charles Collins.

The early years of the life of Isaac Collins were passed in various departments of agriculture, of which he acquired much practical knowledge, ever afterwards retaining a fondness for it. After the death of his father he was placed under the care of his uncle John Hammond, who apprenticed him at the usual age to James Adams, a printer in Wilmington, Delaware, in whose employ he showed great activity and faithfulness. At the request of his master, when in the twentieth year of his age he entered the office of William Rind, at Williamsburg, on James River, Virginia, then the seat of government; he removed to Philadelphia in 1766, and was employed about eighteen months in the printing-office of William Goddard and others. In testimony to his uncommon attention and industry, it may be mentioned that he received a quarter more wages than any other workman in the office.

Here he became acquainted with Joseph Cruikshank, a printer, and afterwards entered into partnership with him. This connection lasted but a short time for want of capital on the part of Isaac Collins, though the friendship of the partners continued through life. The principal work published by them was "The Death of Abel."

In consequence of the death of James Parker, the king's printer for the Province of New Jersey, a new direction was given to the enterprising mind of Isaac

Collins. On hearing of the vacancy, he exclaimed to Joseph Cruikshank, with emotion, "There's a berth for me!" Having obtained letters of recommendation from some of the most influential citizens of Philadelphia, he applied for the position at the next meeting of the Provincial Assembly of New Jersey, in the autumn of 1770, and obtained the appointment of printer to King George III. for the Province of New Jersey. He now felt confident of success, and removed to Burlington, then the seat of government in New Jersey.

A letter addressed by Daniel B. Smith, son of Deborah Smith, second wife of Isaac Collins, to Thomas Stewardson, states that "The tradition among our folks is that John and Samuel Smith, of the King's Council, were drinking tea on the pavement in front of the Wallace House, where John lived, or the Coleman House, where Samuel lived, tradition saith not. A young man, a stranger, in the garb of a Friend, passed along and was greeted by them. He must have impressed them favorably, for they asked him to take tea with them, and made the usual American inquiries. He told them he was a printer in search of a good situation for his business. The brothers talked with each other a while, and then said the colony was in want of a printer, and proposed to him to settle in Burlington, and they would use their influence to get him the office of king's printer. This is understood to have been his first visit to Burlington."

PRINTING-OFFICE

COMMISSION ISSUED TO ISAAC COLLINS AS PRINTER TO THE KING FOR THE PROVINCE OF NEW JERSEY.*

George the Third, by the Grace of God of Great Britain, France and Ireland King, Defender of the Faith.

To all to whom these Presents shall come Greeting:

Know Ye *that we have assigned, constituted and appointed Isaac Collins of the City of Burlington to be our Printer for our Province of New Jersey in America in the place and stead of James Parker Esq., late Printer of our said Province of Nova Caesarea or New Jersey, Together with all Salaries, Fees, Perquisites, Profits, Priviledges and Advantages to the said Office belonging or in any way appertaining, for and during our will and pleasure.*

In testimony whereof We have caused the Great Seal of our said Province to be hereunto affixed.

{L.S.}

---

* The original is in possession of his grandson, Charles Collins, of New York.

Witness our trusty and well-beloved William Franklin Esquire Captain General Governor and Commander in Chief of our said Province of New Jersey and territories thereon depending in America, Chancellor and Vice-Admiral in the same &c at our City of Burlington, the thirtieth day of October, in the eleventh year of our reign Anno Domini, One Thousand seven hundred and seventy.*

Pettit.

Isaac Collins now felt confident of success in his future prospects, and removed to Burlington. Soon after this he married Rachel Budd, a daughter of Thomas and Rebecca Budd, of Philadelphia, to whom he became attached while living in that city. The marriage took place at the Bank Meeting-House, on the 8th of Fifth month, 1771.

THE MARRIAGE CERTIFICATE.

"WHEREAS Isaac Collins, of the City of Burlington in the Province of New Jersey, Printer, son of Charles Collins, late of Newcastle County upon Delaware, deceased, and Rachel Budd of the City of Philadelphia, in the Province of Pennsylvania, daughter of Thomas Budd, late of Bridgetown, in the County of Burlington and Province of New Jersey afores'd, Deceased, Having declared their Intentions

* William Franklin, above referred to, was a son of Benjamin Franklin. He was a good, loyal citizen until the Rebellion occurred, when he deserted the American cause, for which act he was reproved by his father.

BANK MEETING-HOUSE, PHILADELPHIA.

of Marriage with each other before several monthly meetings of the People called Quakers at Philadelphia afores'd, according to the good order used among them & having consent of Parent and Friends concerned, their said proposals were allowed by the said Meeting.

"*Now these are to certify* whom it may concern that for the full accomplishing their said Intentions, this Eighth day of the Fifth month, in the year of our Lord One Thousand Seven Hundred and Seventy one; They the said Isaac Collins & Rachel Budd Appeared in a Public meeting of the said People at Philadelphia Afores'd and the said Isaac Collins taking the s'd Rachel Budd by the Hand, did in a Solemn manner openly Declare that he took her to be his Wife, Promising through the Lord's assistance to be unto her a Loving and Faithful Husband until Death should separate them, and then and there in the same Assembly the s'd Rachel Budd did in like manner declare that she took him the s'd Isaac Collins to be her Husband promising through the Lord's Assistance to be unto him a Loving and Faithful Wife until Death should separate them, and moreover they the s'd Isaac Collins & Rachel Budd (she according to the custom of Marriage Assuming the name of her Husband) as a further confirmation thereof did then and there, to these presents set their hands, And We whose names are here under also Subscribed, being present at the solemnization of the s'd marriage and Subscription, have, as Witnesses thereunto set our hands the day and year above written.

Isaac Collins.

Rachel Collins

JEREMIAH ELFRETH,	ANNA CLIFFORD,
JOSHUA EMLEN,	ELIZABETH SCATTERGOOD,
JOHN PEMBERTON,	REBEKAH BLACKHAM,
SAM. GLANSON,	SUSANNA JONES,
WILLIAM FISHER,	HETTY HEWLINGS, JR.,
CHARLES WEST,	HANNAH MORRIS,

John Elliott,
William Savery,
Thos. Scattergood,
Owen Jones,
Bened't Dorsey,
Jos. Cruikshank,
Thos. Clement,
James Hutchinson,
John Ferris,
Rich. J. Blackham,
Eliza Stevensford,
Sarah Morris,
Mary Pemberton,
Anna Warner,
Sarah Fisher,
Rebecca Scattergood,
Sarah Bartram,
Elizabeth Cooper,
Elizabeth Hartley,
Letitia Powel,
Thos. Say,
Rebekah Say,
Susannah Carmalt,
Elizabeth Bartram,
Elizabeth Collins,
Sarah Bispham,
Mary Barnes,
Stacy Budd,
Joseph Budd,
Benj. Say,
George Wilson, Jr.,
Moses Bartram."

Isaac and Rachel Collins lived in Burlington about seven years in an old-fashioned "hipped-roof" house at the southeast corner of High (or Main) and Union Streets, where four of their children were born. The house still shows on its north side the date of its erection, in large figures. At the time they resided in that "green country town" there were many noted members of the Society of Friends living near by, with some of whom Isaac Collins formed a strong and lasting friendship. The houses were generally built with "stoops," or seated porches, in front, where many a long conversation was held with the neighbors, and not infrequently a cup of tea enjoyed in the open air.

Isaac Collins's business was carried on in a small one-roomed house on High Street, a few doors above Pearl Street, once occupied by Samuel Jennings, first governor of New Jersey, and also used by the Preparative Meeting of Friends of Burlington. The bricks of which it was built were imported from England, while

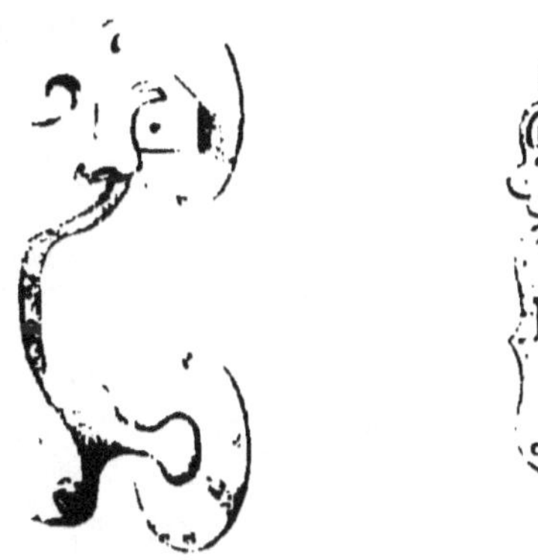

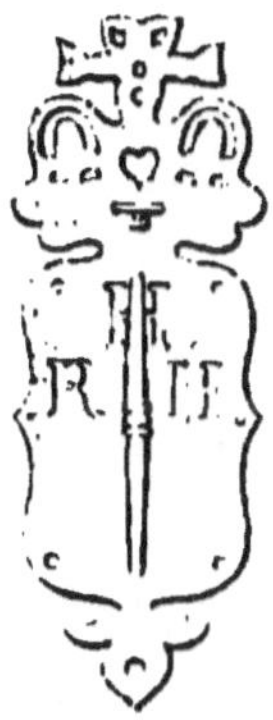

KNOCKER AND DOOR-LATCH FROM ISAAC COLLINS'S PRINTING-OFFICE AT BURLINGTON.

FAC-SIMILE OF PROVINCIAL CURRENCY PRINTED BY ISAAC COLLINS.

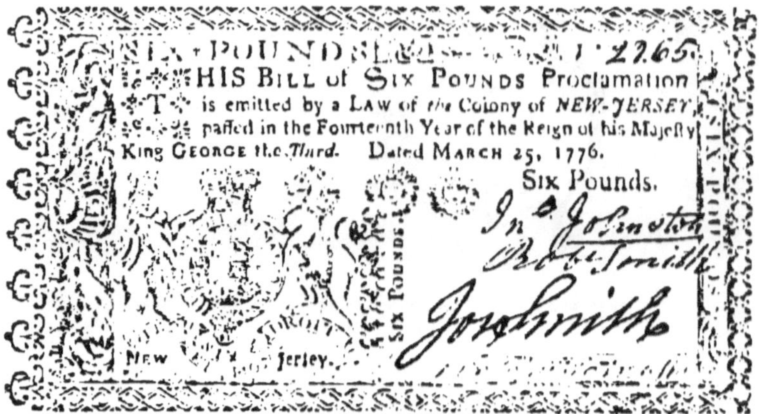

the door-latch, the knocker, and the heavy roof are evidences that this was one of the first houses erected soon after the settlement of Bridlington, afterwards New Beverly, and subsequently Burlington, in 1667. The H. R. H. on the plate of the door-latch, as shown below, are the initials of the first owners, Robert and Hannah Hartshorne. The building was taken down in 1881, the door-latch and knocker being the only relics saved.

In this little house, about twelve by fifteen feet in size, Isaac Collins commenced his successful career as a printer. The first issue from his press was the "New Jersey Almanack," in 1771, continued without interruption for twenty-six years. Following this was the publication of "Laws for the Government," to which succeeded the printing of Sewel's "History of the Rise and Progress of the People called Quakers," a large folio volume of nearly one thousand pages. Of this valuable work two thousand copies were printed. It was issued in 1774. The neatness and correctness of this work obtained for Isaac Collins much credit among Friends, under whose patronage it was executed. In 1776 he printed an edition of one thousand copies of the "Revised Laws of New Jersey," a volume of five hundred pages, and in the same year paper money for the State of New Jersey, to the entire satisfaction of the Legislature. The combination of letter-press and copper-plate printing, and the variety of colors, rendered the notes very difficult to counterfeit.

An edition of three thousand copies of Baxter's "Saint's Everlasting Rest" followed, the work being ordered by the Society of Methodists. After the publication of several smaller works, Isaac Collins issued, in 1777, the first number of the *New Jersey Gazette*, which he continued till 1786.

The quaint old hexagonal meeting-house on High or Main Street, where Isaac Collins met his friends at times of worship, will interest the reader. It was built in 1683, and taken down in 1786–87. The present meeting-house, standing a short distance nearer the street than the old one, was built in 1785. The old buttonwood-trees in the rear of the latter and also in the view of the former may be seen, and consequently must be of great age. It is said that a friendly Indian sachem, or chief, once lived in his wigwam under one of these trees.

In the records of Burlington Monthly Meeting the following minute was found:

"At our Monthly Meeting held at ye house of Thomas Gardiner 12mo. 5, 1682, It is ordered that a Meeting-House be built according to a draft of a six-square building, forty feet square from out to out for which he is to have £160, which ye meeting engageth to see ye persons paid that shall disburse the same unto Francis Collings"

In the spring of 1778, Isaac and Rachel Collins, with their children, removed to Trenton. The printing business was continued by him with increased facilities and more extensive patronage. Besides numerous editions of small books, he printed a new edition of the "Revised Laws of New Jersey," and a "History of the Revolution in South Carolina" in two volumes, octavo, by Dr. Ramsey.

The next work of importance was an edition of five thousand quarto Bibles. The following Prospectus was issued at Trenton, September, 1788:

FRIENDS' MEETING-HOUSE, BURLINGTON.

"PROPOSALS
For printing by subscription the
HOLY BIBLE
containing the Old and New Testaments with the Apocrypha, and
Marginal Notes.
Conditions.

I. This work to be contained in one large volume quarto of nine hundred and eighty five pages, will be printed page for page with the Oxford edition on a beautiful new type and good paper, an index with a concordance—also the scripture measures weights and coins.

II. The price to subscribers for the Volume well-bound Four Spanish Dollars, one dollar to be paid at the time of subscription, the remainder on the delivery of the book.

III. The work to be put to press as soon as three thousand copies shall be subscribed for and to be finished without delay."

At a later date we find this statement made by Isaac Collins:

"Although the subscriptions received are far short of the number proposed the Editor being encouraged by the following extracts, has ventured to begin this work under the hope that many more citizens of America will patronize it especially when they are informed that Dounamie's Concordance which is annexed to Eyre and Strahan's London Quarto Edition of 1772 will be added without further expense to the Subscriber.

"At a meeting for Sufferings Philadelphia 19th of Third month 1789; The subject of the printing of the 'Collins Bible' was discussed and finally it was placed on the record of the Meeting that 'it is the united sense of the meeting that it be recommended to the Quarterly and Monthly meetings of Friends to encourage the work by appointing Committees to procure subscriptions agreeable to the tenor of said Proposals &c.

"Signed, JOHN DRINKER, *Clerk.*"

The General Assembly of the Presbyterian Church in the United States of America, Philadelphia, May 25, 1789.

". . . considered the importance of preserving faithful and correct impressions of the Holy Scriptures and as Mr. Collins, Printer to the State of New Jersey proposes to make an impression of the Old and New Testaments and wishes the countenance and support of all denominations of Christians, on motion,

"*Resolved,*" [Here follows a recommendation to lay Mr. Collins's proposals before their respective Presbyteries, and to procure subscriptions to said work, and sixteen persons were appointed for this purpose.]

"Signed, JAMES F. ARMSTRONG,
"*Clerk of the General Assembly.*"

Extract from the Journal of the Convention of the Protestant Episcopal Church, held in Philadelphia, August 8, 1789:

"*Resolved,* That on motion of Mr. Jones, the members of this Convention will assist Mr. Collins in the procuring of subscriptions."

Extract from the minutes of the Baptist Association, held at Philadelphia, October 6, 1789:

"This Association taking under consideration the proposals of Mr. Isaac Collins of Trenton in New Jersey, Being desirous to encourage so laudable a design, do appoint the Rev. Oliver Hart etc. and moreover the Association recommends to all the churches and congregations in the bounds to assist in the undertaking.

"WILLIAM VAN HORN, *Clerk.*

"A specimen of the type and paper may be seen by applying to Joseph Cruikshank, Printer and Bookseller, in Market street, Philadelphia.

"TRENTON, Twelfth month (Dec.) 19, 1789." *

Although some of his friends had no faith in the project, and endeavored to dissuade him from attempting his greatest work, which he would not abandon, the result did not disappoint him.

---

* *Pennsylvania Gazette*, January 27, 1790.

The work occupied two years, and the result fully satisfied the expectations of the public. Biblical authorities have considered it to be the most correct edition extant. Isaac Collins greatly desired, in undertaking the work, to present to those who had subscribed for it a Bible free from typographical errors, and therefore secured the services of a number of persons who had had long practice in correcting proofs, and who would conscientiously fulfil the arduous task. In revising the proof-sheets, as well as in the examination of various editions of the Bible, several learned and distinguished ministers of different religious denominations gave their aid, while a number of his children assisted in reading the proofs eleven times, the last examination being intrusted to the eldest daughter. A reward of one pound sterling was offered by their father for the detection of any error.

When completed, it was found that the only inaccuracies were a broken letter and in a mark of punctuation.

The copies were sold at the subscription price, and were readily disposed of.

In connection with the above, the following recommendation from Governor Livingston may be of interest:

"*To all whom it may concern:*

"Mr. Isaac Collins has for many years last past been and still is, Printer to the State of New Jersey. Having by this means had the more frequent opportunity to see his works, I have had abundant proof of the accuracy and correctness of his publications, as well as of his remarkable attention to business.

"WIL: LIVINGSTON.

"TRENTON 11 Sept. 1788."

A similar communication was received from David Ramsay.

The proof-sheets of Isaac Collins's Bible were carefully compared with the following: A small quarto Cambridge edition published by John Field, 1666, owned by Dr. Minto, Professor of Mathematics at Princeton College. Both he and Dr. Witherspoon valued it highly for its correctness (see Preface to Trenton edition, last paragraph). The smaller variations were settled by the publisher, aided by James F. Armstrong, a clergyman of Trenton, who referred for the purpose to the original Hebrew and Greek texts. Where greater differences appeared, the proof-sheets were sent to Drs. Witherspoon and Smith, presidents in succession of Princeton College. Additional assistance was obtained from various other denominations.

Four-fifths of the edition were subscribed for by Friends. After Joseph Cruikshank had received the copies he engaged to take, he could not sell other quarto Bibles.

Nearly all the family, including Archibald Bartram, were employed as proof-readers.

The following testimonies to the correctness of the printing deserve notice:

"August, 1790.

"The underwritten have examined the edition of the Holy Scriptures which Mr. Isaac Collins of Trenton is publishing as far as he has proceeded—are highly satisfied with the neatness and accuracy of the work and believe that in the critical attention paid to the different editions of England and Scotland, to the difference of words which are to be found in these editions, and to the care bestowed upon the execution of the whole, the work will be equal to any in the English language.

"Signed, JNO. WITHERSPOON
"SAM S. SMITH
"JAMES F. ARMSTRONG
"OLIVER HART."

The following from the pen of George S. Mott, D.D., is of sufficient interest, historically, to have a place in this history:

"As early as the beginning of the last century laws existed in some of the colonies requiring every family to be furnished with a Bible. This supply continued to be kept up by individual exertion until the meeting of the first Congress, in 1777. To that body a memorial was presented on the Bible destitution throughout the country. This memorial was answered by the appointment of a committee, to advise as to the printing an edition of thirty thousand Bibles. The population of the colonies then was about three millions, and all the Bibles in the entire world at that time did not exceed four millions. This committee reported that the necessary materials, such as paper and types, were so difficult to obtain, that to print and bind thirty thousand copies would cost £10,272 10*s.*, and in their judgment it was impracticable. But they recommended the following:

"'The use of the Bible being so universal, and its importance so great, to direct the Committee on Commerce to import, at the *expense* of Congress, twenty thousand English Bibles from Holland, Scotland, or elsewhere, into the different ports of the States of the Union.' The report was adopted and the importation was ordered.

"In 1781, when the continuance of the war prevented further importation, and there was no telling how long this obstruction might be protracted, the subject of printing the Bible was again urged on Congress, and the matter was referred to a committee of three. On their recommendation the following action was taken:

"'*Resolved*, That the United States, in Congress assembled, highly approve the laudable and pious undertaking of Mr. Robert Aitken, of Philadelphia, as subservient of the interests of religion, and being satisfied of the care and accuracy of the execution of the work, recommend this edition of the Bible to the inhabitants of the United States.'

"This was on September 12, 1782. In 1788, Isaac Collins, a member of the Society of Friends, and an enterprising printer of Trenton, N. J., and who established the first newspaper in that State, issued proposals to print a quarto edition of the Bible in 985 pages, at the price of four Spanish dollars. The Synod of New York and New Jersey, the same year, recommended the undertaking. Dr. Witherspoon, of Princeton, Dr. Samuel Stanhope Smith, President of Nassau Hall, and Rev. Mr. Armstrong, pastor of the Presbyterian church in Trenton, were appointed a committee to concur with committees of any other denominations, or of our own Synods, to revise the sheets, and if necessary, to assist in selecting a standard edition. This committee was also authorized to agree with Mr. Collins to append Ostervald's Notes, if not inconsistent with the wishes of other than Calvinistic subscribers.

"In the spring of 1789 the General Assembly, at its meeting, appointed a committee of sixteen (on which was Mr. Armstrong) to lay Mr. Collins's proposal before their respective Presbyteries, and to recommend that subscriptions be solicited in each congregation. This recommendation was repeated in 1790 and in 1791. Mr. Collins, in 1788, issued an octavo New Testament. The quarto edition of the Bible, thus sustained, was issued in 1791. There were five thousand copies. Ostervald's "Practical Observations," of 170 pages, were furnished to special subscribers, and were bound between the Old and New Testaments. This Bible was so carefully revised that it is still a standard. He and his children read all the proofs. In a subsequent edition, 1793–94, he states in the preface, after mentioning several clergymen who assisted the publisher in 1791: 'Some of these persons, James F. Armstrong in particular, being near the press, assisted also in reading and correcting the proof-sheets.' The above interesting facts on this Collins Bible are found in 'The History of the Presbyterian Church, Trenton, N. J.,' by Dr. John Hall, the pastor. The care that was taken by Mr. Collins is evident from the closing paragraph of the preface.

"'The publisher has only further to add that he has made the following impression from the Oxford edition of 1784, by Jackson and Hamilton, and has been particularly attentive in the revisal and correction of the proof-sheets with the Cambridge edition of 1688, by John Field, with the Edinburgh edition of 1775 by Kincaid, and, in all variations, with the London edition of 1772 by Eyre and Strahan—that where there was any difference in words, or in the omission or addition of words, among these he followed that which appeared to be most agreeable to the Hebrew of Arias Montanus, and to the Greek of Arias Montanus and Leufden, without permitting himself to depart from some one of the above-mentioned

English copies, unless in the mode of spelling, in which he has generally followed Johnson.'

"At the end of the New Testament is arranged an Index, or more accurately, an Epitome of the Old and New Testaments, with a Chronological Table in parallel columns. Following this are tables of Scripture weights, measures, and coins; of offices and conditions of men; and the old table of kindred and affinity. The volume closes with a Concordance, 'carefully perused and enlarged by John Dounamie, B.A.' This Concordance is not so full as Cruden's, but is very serviceable. The 'Practical Observations' by Ostervald take up each chapter separately, giving first a brief explanation and then observations much after the manner of Doddridge. The remarks, even in the Epistle to the Romans, are evangelical, rather than Calvinistic, and contain little that would be objected to by an Armenian. This Ostervald was a 'Professor of Divinity, and one of the ministers of the church in Neufchâtel, Switzerland.'

"The copy before me was presented to the Presbyterian church in Flemington, N. J., which was organized in 1791. It was used as the pulpit Bible for sixty-six years. It was the gift of Jasper Smith, one of the ruling elders and President of the Board of Trustees. He was an ardent patriot of the Revolution, a devoted Christian, and a strong Presbyterian. At the time he was one of the leading lawyers of the county. To his exertions and his generous contributions was mainly due the organization of the church, which is now approaching the close of its first century. About the beginning of this century Mr. Smith removed to Lawrenceville, N. J., where he died. In his will he bequeathed to the Presbyterian church there the large farm of over two hundred acres, which is now the manse farm. This Bible of Collins is not only the first, but so far as I know, the only edition of the Holy Scriptures printed in New Jersey."

Isaac Collins published a weekly paper styled the *New Jersey Gazette.* The first number was issued December 5, 1777, at Burlington; then the printing was transferred to Trenton the next year. This was the first paper of the kind published in the State. The British army at that time having possession of Philadelphia, the paper was printed in Trenton until 1786. It was established to counteract the anti-republican tendency of Rivington's *Royal Gazette*, in New York. Governor Livingston, of New Jersey, was a correspondent of the *New Jersey Gazette* as long as it remained in the hands of Isaac Collins. As it was published during the eventful period of the Revolutionary War, and in the vicinity of some of its operations, he was much occupied by the business of the government, and conducted the paper, which was much sought for, as it was published in the neighborhood of scenes of conflict, containing correct information of the movements both of the royal and revolutionary forces.

From the commencement of the arduous struggle for national independence, Isaac Collins was a firm supporter of the rights of his country. So strong and active an interest did he take therein, both in publishing and in private life, that his fellow-members among the Friends finally disowned him. It was not long, however, before, on mature reflection, Friends, missing his valuable services, reinstated him in their Meeting on his statement that he would like again to be in fellowship with them, and he subsequently became clerk of the Chesterfield Quarterly Meeting, which was held at Trenton.

As editor of the *New Jersey Gazette* he was asked to communicate to the Legislative Council the name of the author of an article that appeared in the *Gazette* over the signature of Cincinnatus.

"TRENTON PRINTING OFFICE,
"October 30th, 1779.

"GENTLEMEN,—The Clerk of the Council delivered to me yesterday, a resolution of your hon. House, dated Trenton Council Chamber, October 29th, 1779, requiring me immediately to inform the Council who the author of the publication inserted in the *New Jersey Gazette*, No. 96, under the signature of 'Cincinnatus,' is, and at whose request the same was published.

"Were I to comply with the requisition contained in this resolution, without the permission of the author of the piece alluded to, I conceive I should betray the trust reposed in me, and be far from acting as a faithful guardian of the Liberty of the Press. I may further say, that I am entirely at a loss to conjecture upon what ground this requisition has been made; for it is evident that the piece in question does not contain the most distant disrespectful allusion to your honorable body.

"For the above reasons, gentlemen, I find myself under the disagreeable necessity of declining to comply with your orders. In any other case, not incompatible with good conscience or the welfare of my country, I shall think myself happy in having it in my power to oblige you.

"I am, gentlemen, yours very respectfully,

"ISAAC COLLINS.

"To the Hon. Legislative Council of the State of N. J."

"HOUSE OF ASSEMBLY,
"October 29th, 1779.

"The House of Assembly having taken into consideration the message from Council of yesterday by Mr. Talman, relative to a certain piece published in the *New Jersey Gazette*, No. 96, signed 'Cincinnatus,'

"*Resolved*, That this House do not concur in the resolution therein contained.

"*Ordered*, That Mr. Smock and Mr. Nelson do wait on the Council, and acquaint them therewith.

"By order of the House,

"M. EWING, JR., *Clerk*."

"LIBERTY OF THE PRESS."

It may be proper to introduce here the following by Isaac Collins:

"Whether the Liberty of the Press ought to extend so far as to justify the publishing the Name of a Person with Strictures on his conduct by an anonymous Author or with a fictitious Signature?

"'The Liberty of the Press,' says an excellent Writer, whose sentiments upon this subject I have long since adopted, has ever been esteemed by all free Nations as their grand Bulwark against the abuse of Office, the Oppression of Men in Power and publick Peculation and publick Mismanagement of every Sort. The People at large, generally immersed in their own domestick Occupations, think that all goes well while they hear Nothing to the contrary. They advert but little to Politicks; and, after having appointed the different Officers to transact the Affairs of the Commonwealth, they think that every Thing goes right, because it ought to do so. There are nevertheless a thousand Ways in which they may be abused in the Confidence they may repose, and respecting which they ought to be obliged to any Man who will be at the Trouble to undeceive them. The Press hath always been found a most excellent Instrument for this Purpose. It is the easiest Channel that can be contrived, thro' which to communicate to the People the danger to which they are exposed. To shew them *that* they are, and *how* they are imposed upon by those who betray their Confidence, and by these Means to unite them in removing the Grievance and procuring themselves Justice. This Channel of Communication, having ever been found so salutary to Liberty and so formidable to publick Corruption, has been the constant Darling of the Virtuous and the perpetual Dread of the Wicked. Hence Despotic Governments * inhibit Printing altogether. Arbitrary States † generally lay it under such Restrictions as nearly amount to a Prohibition: And even some Constitutions,‡ that loudly vaunt of Liberty and Law, have often so shackled and hampered it as to render it relative to the two greatest and most important subjects that can occupy the Human Mind and which most essentially affect our present and future Felicity, I mean Religion and Government, almost totally useless. But, Thanks to Heaven! the Americans entertain very different Sentiments about the Liberty of the Press. They have, and, as inseparably with the Idea of Freedom, they must have, a Right to publish the Conduct of their Superiors, in order to communicate it to their Fellow Citizens for facilitating the Remedy and correcting the Mischiefs—All that a Writer in this Case is to look to, is, that his Accusations be true, or at least so probably founded that he cannot be supposed to

---

* Turkish Empire. † Spain. ‡ France.

be instigated by Malevolence. Are we not then under Obligations to every Writer who will point out all those whose particular Conduct deserves to be criminated? And must a Man who is willing to devote a Portion of his Time, thus essentially to serve his Country and thereby save it from Destruction that *must* otherwise *inevitably* happen, be *obliged* to set his *Name* to his *Publications?* An Author may have *many* Reasons for writing under a *fictitious* Signature. Though willing to serve his Fellow Citizens by communicating his Sentiments about publick Men and publick Measures as an anonymous Writer, he would be totally discouraged from doing it, were he obliged to reveal his Name. He may distrust his Capacity for correct Composition and dread the Ridicule of ill-natured Criticks. He may fear to draw upon himself the personal Animosity of those whose Conduct he holds up to publick View and embroil himself with all their Connections. He may be too much above or too much below the level of those whose Conduct he criminates, to enter with them on equal Terms into personal Altercation. At any Rate why should he be made the Butt of their united Vengeance, when his sole Object is to serve the Community? Sometimes his Publications may lose the Effect they would otherwise have produced merely from his being known to be the Author. Can it be expected that a Writer of a Course of Speculations on political Subjects will continue to write under such Circumstances? And have not a thousand Essays been published under borrowed Names? We all know there have and personall Attacks too. And what Necessity for this puerile Inquisitiveness? Is a Man's Reasoning either the better or the worse for its being communicated without a Name? Can we not embrace Truth and reject Error without knowing the Christian and Surname of the Person who writes it? If we do not know *who* he is, which is of no Consequence at all, we shall soon know *what* he is from the *Nature* of his Publications.

"Hence it is evident that anonymous Authors are not only justifiable in reprobating publick Measures and the Conduct of publick Men when they see them going counter to the *Commonweal*, but deserve the *highest* Approbation and Applause of their Fellow-Citizens. But it is urged that using of Names on these Occasions can be of no use and may be of real Detriment. It is admitted on all Hands that we have an undoubted Right to designate a Character in *such* a *Manner* as to identify the Person (and indeed any Thing short of this would be perfect Nonsense) *where then*, in the Name of Common Sense is the Difference? I cannot conceive that any Man of Understanding and Reflection, when he coolly considers the Matter, can seriously advance such an Opinion. In short it appears to me a Shadow without a Substance—Words without a Meaning—and a mere Mark of Timidity in the Writer. Pray, what would be the Consequence of such a Doctrine? It would be Nothing less than this—that no Man in a little Time would dare either to find Fault with publick Men or publick Measures—because, this Doctrine, once established would put it in the Power of any publick Man to say he was the Person pointed at, or the Legislature, however ridiculous their Proceedings might be, to declare these were unjustifiable Reflections against them and therefore he or they of Right would demand the name of the Author in order to wreak their Vengeance upon him. This Doctrine is so ridiculous that it is even exploded by the corrupt and infatuated People of England. Since which Nothing is more common in that Country than to see fictitious Authors levelling all their Artillery against not only Ministers of State by Name but even against their King himself. And is there an American who possesses a sentiment less free? I trust there is not. There *cannot* be. 'Tell it not in Gath—publish it not in the streets of Ascalon! lest the Philistines rejoice—lest the uncircumcised triumph!' *

"The Licentiousness of the Press is sufficiently checked, in the first Place, by the Printer's Reputation, Interest and Loss, and, secondly, by his being amenable to the Laws of his Country for any *wanton*, *false*, or *malicious* Attacks he may admit in his Paper against the Government itself or against the publick or private Character of any Individual in it. And more or less than this I would never wish to see established in any of the United States of America.

"TRENTON, March 20, 1784."

The following from Isaac Collins, addressed to Governor William Livingston on the "Freedom of the Press," is sufficiently interesting to warrant its introduction here.

* 2 Samuel i. 20.

ISAAC COLLINS, OF TRENTON, NEW JERSEY, TO GOVERNOR WILLIAM LIVINGSTON.

"TRENTON, N. J., March 6, 1781.

"RESPECTED FRIEND,—

"The Time was, and I recollect it with Pleasure, when I felt myself obliged as a Citizen by your Friendship and Acquaintance; when I flattered myself that I had your entire Approbation and good Wishes in my Profession; and when as Publisher of the *New Jersey Gazette* I could not but be highly sensible of the advantages it derived from your Encouragement, Attention and Support. An unfortunate Publication in this Paper which through the eager and excessive Resentment of some drew after it consequences much against my Inclination, gave a very different appearance to Things. I apprehend this to be the cause of the alteration of Conduct which has Place, as I cannot otherwise account for it. By the advice of Friends in whose Candor and good Sense I have Confidence, and Conscious of the best Intentions I am led to make use of this means to do away every cause of Estrangement and Disgust.

"In the Conduct of a News Paper no Man, I believe, is more desirous, or more in the custom of taking the Advice and Sentiments of such as are reported knowing and best affected to the Principles of Liberty, but so notwithstanding as to support my own Independence of Judgement and Practice. My Ear is open to every Man's Instruction but to no Man's influence. You yourself would despise me for having no opinion of my own. I have ever maintained a Sovereign Respect for the Freedom of the Press, as far as I have been able of comprehending the Nature of it. If I have at any Time been mistaken in this Respect, those who know me best will most readily declare that I have waited only for Correction to alter what was wrong. Difference of opinion is a common thing but I deny and scorn the Imputation of being wilfully in an Error.

"The motives of the writer of the Piece adverted to are with himself; for my part I will only say that no Shadow either of Disaffection or Indifference to the Interests of my Country, no personal Dislike or Disrespect had any share in my Conduct. I can scarcely bear to take notice of such an Insinuation though I know some went so far as to make it. My whole Behavior is and ever has been a direct Contradiction to every Thing of this kind.

"As a Christian, as a Citizen of New Jersey, as one who is desirous of being useful to the Cause of Liberty and Virtue I have thought it my duty to explain these Circumstances, and the difference of station points out the propriety of my making the first Declaration. I am free to profess I shall never decline any means of removing a subsisting Uneasiness and Misunderstanding provided they are not unworthy of an Independent Citizen conscious of having done intentional Injury to no man. It shall not be my fault if I have not the Satisfaction to see the Governor as heretofore and on the Terms which were so beneficial to the Publick and agreeable to myself."

The following sufficiently illustrate the value of the services rendered by Isaac Collins:

From Minutes of the Provincial Congress and the Council of Safety of New Jersey.

ASSEMBLY OF NEW JERSEY.

"PERTH AMBOY, Feb. 6, 1775.

"*Resolution* 16, To Isaac Collins, or any other Printer, hereafter to be appointed, for printing the Minutes of the House of Representatives, of any sitting during the continuance of this Act, and for printing the Laws passed at any sitting as aforesaid, or any other printing, such sums as Hendrick Fisher, Stephen Crane, James Kinsey, and Thomas Polgreen Howlings, Esquires, or any two of them shall agree to be paid for such service."

PROVINCIAL CONGRESS OF NEW JERSEY.

"TRENTON, October 28, 1775.

"*Resolved*, That as soon as the Secretary hath prepared a fair copy of the minutes of this Congress for the press, Mr. President do issue an order to Isaac Collins, to immediately print off one thousand copies thereof, for the use of the Colony in general; and five hundred copies of the new Militia Ordinance, with the Articles of War, for regulating the Continental army, annexed, for the use of the Militia forces."

"COMMITTEE OF SAFETY, PRINCETON, September 14, 1775.

"*Ordered*, That Joseph Borden and Enos Kelsey be a Committee to employ Isaac Collins to print the Minutes of the Provincial Congress of New Jersey; as also such Proceedings of the Committee of Safety as to them may appear necessary."

Acts of the Legislature of New Jersey, Chapter LXVII., passed December 9, 1777.

"WHEREAS it is absolutely necessary that the Laws of this State should from Time to Time be printed with all possible Dispatch after passing the same and whereas Isaac Collins, who is appointed to print the said Laws, hath represented to the said Legislature that he cannot carry the said Business into Execution, or fulfil his Contract to print and publish a weekly News Paper in the State unless he and the Workmen employed therein are exempted from actual service in the Militia.

"SEC. 1. Be it therefore Enacted by the Council and General Assembly of this State, and it is hereby Enacted by the Authority of the same, that the said Isaac Collins, and any number of men, not exceeding four to be employed by him in his Printing Office, shall be and they hereby are exempted from actual service in the Militia during the term they shall be so employed; provided that the men so exempted be furnished with Arms, Ammunition and Accoutrements as directed by the Act entitled 'An Act for the better regulation of the Militia,' and that they be subject to be called into active service on a Call of the Militia, when the County in which they are employed shall be actually invaded."

New Jersey Archives, Volume X., page 731.

GOVERNOR WILLIAM FRANKLIN TO THE LEGISLATURE OF NEW JERSEY.

[Extract.]

"BURLINGTON, June 22, 1776.

". . . Finding that the Provincial Congress had published some of their resolves respecting me, but kept back others, I determined to publish my letter to you which contained the whole of them, at least all which had come to my hands. For this purpose I sent a copy to a Mr. Isaac Collins, who holds a Commission as Printer for this province. But though he at first gave me expectations that he would do his duty (as all good Officers ought to do, or resign their commissions) he afterwards returned it, declaring that he was afraid of offending the Provincial Congress, and that he did not doubt but he should be killed if he should print it for me, with many more excuses of like nature. I desired a person to tell him that my name, being subscribed in my own hand to the paper, would be a sufficient justification for him and ought to remove all his fears of personal danger; and as to myself I was perfectly indifferent to the consequences, it being a rule with me to do the duty of my station and leave the event to Providence. Whether he thought from the specimen the Congress had already given in my Case that he ought not to trust to either their reason or justice and that the more honestly he acted the greater would be the offence and punishment or whether he had a secret bias towards their measures, I cannot say: But certain it is, no argument could prevail, and he returned the copy. I have since heard that he (contrary to my express orders) communicated it to some persons, by which means it came to the knowledge of the Congress, who passed a Resolve this day, prohibiting the printing anything for me,—Poor men! They can no more bear the light of truth, it seems, than Owls can endure the light of the sun!"

New Jersey Archives, Volume X., page 358.

"At a Council held at Burlington February 21 1772

"His Excellency was pleased to sign the following Warrants ordering the Treasurers, or either of them to pay

"872 To Isaac Collins Esquire for printing the Laws & Votes of the last Session of General Assembly and other Services, agreeably to the Certificate of Abraham Howlings and Henry Paxson Esquires

"£153.15.3"

New Jersey Archives, Volume X., page 270.

JOHN HART TO GOVERNOR WILLIAM LIVINGSTON.

"PRINCETOWN, Nov. 25, 1777.

"SIR,—The House of Assembly Request that your Excellency Direct Mr. Collings to print Fifty Copies of the Law for purching

Cloathing for the New Jersey Redgment and transmit the same to your Excellency as soon as possable. I am Sir

"Youre Humble Sevant

"JOHN HART."

Although Isaac Collins had not enjoyed the advantages of perhaps a very liberal education, his occupation strengthened a desire for the improvement of his mind, and during his residence in Trenton he, with a number of persons, formed a society for the purpose of improvement in composition. Some of the essays read at the meetings are still extant, each endorsed with the writer's name.

Another object still dearer to him was the education of his fourteen children, of whom seven sons and six daughters survived him, one daughter having died in infancy. He accordingly united with some of the most respectable citizens of Trenton in founding an academy for the education of the young people of that place. He not only subscribed liberally to it, but paid for the tuition of nine of his children (all who were old enough to attend), although his subscription entitled him to their free instruction. This seminary of learning was ably conducted, the classical branches being taught by distinguished professors. In testimony to his exertions in organizing and conducting the school, we append the following:

"At a meeting of the Proprietors of the Trenton Academy on the 8th day of February 1798:

"*Resolved* unanimously that Isaac Collins, late one of the Trustees of their Academy, for his exertions in its first Institution and his unwearied diligence in its Establishment and Support is entitled to the thanks of the Proprietors.

"*Ordered* that the Clerk transmit a Copy of this Resolution to the said Isaac Collins by the first opportunity.

"A true copy of the minutes.

"JOS. BRUMLEY."

"*To the Proprietors of the Trenton Academy:*

"GENTLEMEN,—I received in due Season and with much Pleasure your note of Thanks for my exertions in the first Institution and for the Establishment of the Trenton Academy.

"As no temporal matter was nearer my heart while I had the Pleasure of residing among you, than the welfare and Success of this Seminary, so, nothing could be more gratifying than this Expression of your Approbation for any little services I may have rendered the Institution. That it may long flourish under your Patronage with a vigilant Board of Trustees is the ardent wish of, Gentlemen

"your very respectful Friend

"ISAAC COLLINS.

"NEW YORK, 4 mo. 28, 1798."

"'The Trenton School Company' originated in a meeting of citizens held February 10, 1781. The original capital was seven hundred and twenty dollars, divided into thirty-six shares. Part of the lot still occupied by the academy in Hanover (then Fourth) Street was purchased, and a stone building erected, one story of which was occupied in 1782. The next year it was enlarged and the endowment increased. In 1785 it was incorporated, and in 1794 its funds were aided by a lottery. In 1800 the girls' school of the academy was removed to the school-house belonging to the Presbyterian Church." *

At this academy seven of the children of Isaac Collins were educated, and the following certificate, awarded to his eldest son, shows the character of the studies required:

* "History of the Presbyterian Church at Trenton, New Jersey," by John Hall, D.D.

"To the Superintendent and Trustees of Trenton Academy:

"*To all to whom these Presents may come, Greeting:*

"*Be it known* that Charles Collins of Trenton, hath regularly studied the following subjects in this Academy, viz; Arithmetic, Geography, and the English Language grammatically, Cæsar's Commentaries, Sallust, Virgil, Cicero's Orations and Horace in Latin—with the New Testament, Lucian, Xenophon and Homer in Greek.

"And after sufficient public examination previously had, hath been approved as having obtained a competent skill in each of these Studies, and hath during the course of his studies supported a good moral character and conducted himself with Exemplary Respect and Subjection to the Officers and Laws of this Institution.

"In Testimony whereof the Common Seal of the Corporation is [SEAL.] hereunto affixed and our Names subscribed.

"James F. Armstrong, Sup.
"Jas. Ewing
"Moore Furman
"Conrad Kotts
"Isaac Collins
"Maskell Ewing

"Given at a public examination in the said Academy on the 16th day of September 1789."

The newspapers of that day tell of the "crowded and polite audiences" which attended, usually including the Governor, Legislature, and distinguished strangers. Among the latter, in 1784, were the President of Congress, the Baron Steuben, etc. A full history of the academy down to 1847 may be found in ten successive numbers of the *State Gazette* of April and May of that year.

There was a paper-mill in Trenton before the time of the publication of Collins's Bible. In December, 1788, it was advertised by its proprietors, Stacy Potts and John Reynolds, as "now nearly completed." The manufacturers issued earnest appeals for rags; in one of their publications presenting to the "consideration of those mothers who have children going to school the present great scarcity of that useful article without which their going to school would avail but little."

The printing and publishing business, with the sales of stationery, was carried on by the family for many years.

In 1799 Isaac Collins opened a printing-office at 189 Pearl Street, New York, and in 1802, with his son Thomas, engaged in business as booksellers. In 1805 he took into partnership Benjamin W. Perkins, Jr., under the firm name of Collins, Perkins & Co., but in 1808 retired, leaving the business to Collins (Thomas) & Perkins. After the death of B. W. Perkins, the firm was changed to Collins & Co., and the business carried on by some of the sons of Isaac Collins, at the same place, until 1822, when the youngest son, Joseph B., moved to 117 Maiden Lane. He had been associated for one or two years with his brother Benjamin (B. & J. Collins) as stereotypers in Spring Street.* Benjamin commenced business as bookseller, in company with Samuel Hannay, at 230 Pearl Street, in 1817, but withdrew from the firm in 1832, the business being continued by S. Hannay and George B. Collins, the only son of Charles Collins.

* The first stereotyping done in this country was by the firm of Collins (Thomas), Perkins & Co., employing for this purpose an Englishman named John Watt, and the first book for which such plates were used was Lindley Murray's English Grammar. It is said that Benjamin S. Collins paid five thousand dollars for the process, at that time a secret.

In 1835 Benjamin S. and Stacy B. Collins were associated, and continued together at 230 Pearl Street, under the firm name of B. & S. Collins, and with John Keese as Collins, Keese & Co. In 1838 they moved to 254 Pearl Street, where the business was carried on for nearly thirty years by the old partners and the sons of Benjamin, the firms being Collins, Keese & Co., 1836–38; Collins, Brother & Co., 1838–42; Collins & Brother, 1842–47; Robert B. Collins, 1847–50. In 1857 Collins & Brother (R. B. C. and C. C.) moved to the west side of the city. In 1884 Robert B. Collins withdrew from the firm, and shortly after Charles Collins retired from the general business, and has since confined himself to the publication of a few text-books.

From the record of the public and official life of Isaac Collins it may be well to turn to some notices of his domestic relations. All of those who were coeval with him and his beloved consort have passed away, and there remain only a few reminiscences.

REMINISCENCES

BY MARIA S. REEVE, DAUGHTER OF RICHARD M. AND SUSANNA R. SMITH.

"It is declared by Solomon, who is said to have been the wisest of men, that 'the glory of children are their fathers,' and we meet this evening to memorize our virtuous, honorable ancestors. I feel that I can add but little to the information already produced; but, living near our grandfather in his later years, I have a vivid recollection of his personal appearance. He was a little above the medium height, somewhat taller than any of his sons, dignified and rather reserved in manner. I remember him as one to be somewhat feared, perhaps at the same time warmly loved, and I thought it a great privilege to be allowed to wait upon him. On his last visit at my father's he was seized with an ague, and I well remember my mother bidding me—at this time five years old—bring a chair and assist her in warming a blanket to spread over him as he lay upon the sofa drawn close to the fire, and the pride and pleasure I felt in doing it impressed my young mind forcibly.

"I have often regretted that some of us of this generation had not enough curiosity to inquire more fully of our parents of their ancestry. My dear mother used to tell me what one of her friends, much older than herself, told her of her parents at the time of their marriage. Our grandmother, it seems, was very beautiful, lovely both in mind and person. Her daughter Elizabeth resembled her more than any of her fair-haired daughters. Her wedding-dress was a light blue brocade, made in the fashion of the day,—robe style, with one hoop and very long in the back,—a short blue bodice with a white satin stomacher in front in the shape of a heart, embroidered in colors, with a blue silk cord laced across from side to side attaching it to the bodice, which was very elegant. Shoes of the same material as the dress, pointed at the toe and with very high heels, not much larger at the sole than a gold dollar. To crown this dress she placed on her head a black hood lined with white, and a huge cape extending over her shoulders. On her return from the meeting-house where they were married, she laid aside her hood and donned a white apron of large dimensions, of a thin gauzy material tied with a wide blue ribbon, and large bow in front, below.

"Now for the groom! (My mother used to tell me of what her friends told her with so much *pride*, I might almost say.) He was dignified in manner and *good looking*. His wedding garb was of fine cloth of a *peach-blossom color*. Coat with large skirt and outside front pockets, lined throughout with white silk elaborately quilted, large vest of same material, 'small clothes,' with silver knee-buckles, white silk stockings and pumps, crowned with a handsome *three-cornered beaver*. (I find, in looking over the account of the marriage of Governor Logan's daughter to my great-grandfather, that the same style of dress was worn by her, even to the apron.

"Their manner of living was simple, as my mother used to say, the many children that soon flocked around them taking their meals upon a long table fastened to the wall of the dining-room. At night the supper consisted solely of bread and milk, or mush and milk, which was eaten standing, none being allowed to sit till they were old enough to be admitted to the table of their parents.

"My mother often spoke of the tender affection which existed between them. The gallantry of her father as he would come into the nursery and take the needle-work from her hands, place her bonnet upon her head, and take her a nice ride to refresh her motherhood; also mentioning how he would come in and empty his silk handkerchief, filled with Spanish dollars, into her lap, to the astonishment of the little ones around them. His word was like the law of the Medes and Persians,—there was no revoking it. When he came in fatigued with the business of the day and found half a dozen merry little girls and boys having a good time with their dear mother, if he raised his finger, the room was cleared in a moment, and after a half-hour's rest he would say, 'The horse will be at the door in ten minutes, and we will take a ride;' and most careful was she not to keep him waiting. This was one of the many valuable lessons she taught her girls, telling them 'always to remember that the time of the master was more important than that of any one else, seeing they all depended on him for support.'

"My mother, several of the sisters, and some of the little boys attended a school kept by an elderly French lady they called 'Madame.' In sending out school bills for the quarter it was her invariable practice to add this item, viz.:

"'For manners . . . . *6d.*'

"Her principal instruction was in plain sewing, and her discipline was excellent. Her success in teaching needle-work was remarkable, for, under her care, my mother, at the age of seven years, had completed a set of six fine linen shirts for her father, all made by her own little fingers. She used to tell how pleased her parents were when she took them home, and how every hem and button-hole was examined and commended.

"After 'Madame's' reign was over, mother and several of the older children were sent to 'The Academy' at Trenton. Charles Ewing, afterwards Governor of New Jersey, was a student there in the same Latin class, where my mother was the only girl. A mutual fancy for each other was the result, but in after-life their paths diverged.

"Their cousin, Archibald Bartram, was another of the many admirers of the young ladies, but the near relationship prevented an escapade with one of the youngest maidens, their father keeping a close watch upon all intruders.

"But in the midst of their happiness and prosperity came, in after-years, the terrible blow in the death of the darling wife and beloved mother, which seemed for a while almost to paralyze them. After this sad event several of the daughters were solicited to take part in teaching in Nine Partners Boarding-School, my mother being one of them. Two of the sisters kept house in New York City for two or more of their brothers.

"By this time our grandfather had become a plain Friend, taking part in the affairs of the church, etc. After having removed to Burlington, New Jersey, he married my father's aunt, who was the widow of Benjamin Smith, and had two children (Daniel B. and Margaret M. Smith). The families lived together under his roof in the greatest harmony, Daniel B. Smith and Stacy B. Collins being much united, 'like own brothers,' as mother would say.

"In a few years our dear ancestor passed away in much peace, though in great physical suffering. After this event his widow retired with her two children to her own house in Burlington.

"Although there are few relics left of the married life of Isaac and Rachel Collins, they have left us what is far better than silver or gold or fine apparel, unsullied 'footprints on the sands of time.' May we be stimulated to follow them in all that is right and good and true.

"Fifth month, 1892."

From Rachel S. Howland, of New Bedford, Second Daughter of Richard M. and Susanna R. Smith.

"After our father's death in 1826, when the feelings of loneliness came heavily upon the much-reduced household, mother would often interest us with recollections of her early life, recalling characteristics of her parents. The utter dismay and deep grief of the stricken family were especially dwelt upon. The expression of her father on this occasion (not very cheering or comforting to the poor bereaved children) was, 'I had rather have lost all my property and all my children than that their mother should have died!'

"He certainly was a stern, not to say a severe, man in his family, and yet with his strong sense of duty he was very desirous of providing educational advantages for them and giving his sons a good start in business. His social position was of the best; an excellent provider, his table was always well supplied, and, during their life in Trenton especially, so many Friends made his house their temporary home that it came to bear the title of the 'Quaker Tavern.' Our Aunt Rebecca Grellet was his favorite child, and when the young Étienne, the French refugee, had the temerity to ask him for her hand, the favor was most unwillingly granted, and only after much conflict and much consideration.

"Grandfather was very neat and tasty in his dress. His fine Holland linen and his peach-blossom vests and short clothes with white silk or thread stockings were the admiration of his daughters; and when he made an evening call, the good-wives of his acquaintance were wont to say, 'Here comes Mr. Collins. We know him by his carefulness in scraping and wiping his shoes upon the mat as he enters.'

"The children were sent at three years old to Madame Dunbar's school, and some of them kept there till they were thirteen, when they were transferred to the Trenton Academy, which our grandfather was largely instrumental in founding, in which work he was assisted by Chief-Justice Ewing, his most intimate friend, whose son, Charles Ewing, was the children's playmate and associate in those classic halls.

"My mother was a fair Latin scholar, and greatly enjoyed the ability this gave her to explain to us the derivation of words in common use from their ancient roots. In conducting the printing business her father employed his daughters frequently as proof-sheet readers, and thus they became very accurate in spelling and reading; and in the preparation of the great quarto Bible, the first English one of that size published in this country, they obtained an intimate knowledge of the Scriptures, as they were obliged to read large portions of it several times over, and the publisher received high encomiums on the remarkable accuracy of the edition.

"As an instance of the home training of the children in instant obedience, mother would tell us that when they were gathered around the family fireside in the evening, if a visitor was announced, their father had only to raise his hand and point his finger to the door, when the whole troop would depart without a word of protest or murmur of regret.

"Madame Dunbar, the French lady, must have been an excellent disciplinarian as well as instructor in the elementary branches of learning. She had two methods of punishment. The children were seated on long forms or benches, and if they struggled against the inevitable weariness consequent on their constrained position so vigorously as to fall perceptibly out of line, madame would call for her long rod and quickly lay it across the laps of the whole row, reminding them of their error. The other thing they dreaded was the appearance of the great gray wig, which was kept within reach, and when a child was naughty it was whirled through the air and with a good and sure aim came plump upon the delinquent, whose duty it was to carry it through the room to madame, who forthwith placed it upon the head of the offender, who was made to stand up beside the desk or throne of the much-feared potentate.

"Madame's skill in using and teaching the girls the use of the needle was phenomenal. It was a proud day for my mother as well as for her teacher when she carried home the shirt made by herself and folded by her instructor, with all the seams pounded into perfect flatness with a special little hammer provided for the purpose. The little maiden received from her revered parent a great Spanish silver dollar as a token of his approbation. Subsequently she made up for him a whole piece of the same fine Holland linen.

"Before I came to the age of intelligent observation my father must have died. Therefore I do not know how he looked; but the portrait now in the possession of the family must be a good likeness, for I have heard my mother say that when it was carried home from the studio the boys ran after it, shouting, 'There goes Mr. Collins!'

"The oil-painting, by Jarvis, was taken after he had become a plain 'Friend,' which was not very early in life.*

"In order that his children might enjoy the advantages of a guarded religious education and more social intercourse with members of the religious Society of Friends, Isaac Collins purchased a house in the city of New York, and removed there with his family

---

* After the death of Rachel Collins a portrait-painter was requested to meet with the family and endeavor to make a likeness from the description given by the members. It is almost needless to say that he was unsuccessful. J. C.

in 1796, Rebecca, his eldest child, being then twenty-four, and the youngest, Joseph Budd Collins, two years of age.

"He continued to print and publish many useful works while in that city, including large editions of Lindley Murray's excellent Grammars and School Readers, the Introduction, English Reader and Sequel. All these were very popular at that time. The purity of style and the moral tendency of the latter have never been surpassed in more modern text-books.

"In addition to his printing business he was persuaded to go into partnership with his eldest son in the importation and sale of broadcloths, expecting ample returns from the capital thus invested; but, finding his hard-earned property fast vanishing in the new business, he abandoned it after the loss of thousands of dollars, and devoted his sole attention to his former occupation. By this judicious change in his plans he found himself, in a few years, in independent circumstances, and then wisely retired from the busy scenes of life.

"During the prevalence of the yellow fever in the city of New York in the years 1798, 1799, 1801, 1803, and 1805 he removed to the country with his large family, to be, if possible, beyond the reach of infection. Not to be unemployed, he always took with him sufficient printing materials to continue his business to advantage and give his sons and daughters some employment. It was in the last-mentioned of these years that our grandfather suffered the deepest affliction of all his life. His beloved wife, after a few days' illness, died of yellow fever at West Farms, twelve miles from New York City, in the fifty-fifth year of her age. As an expression of her great worth and excellence of character, we make the following extract from the testimony of the bereaved husband, written a short time after her decease:

"'My dearly beloved wife was the child of those who feared God and worked righteousness. They were excellent in precept and example, and she "followed them as they followed Christ." We lived together in much harmony more than thirty-four years. She was endowed with a strong mind, of quick discernment, and had an extraordinarily retentive memory, was of a sweet disposition and lively imagination, guarded in her conversation and humble in her deportment, very benevolent and the friend of the poor.

"'Having a large number of children, her time and talents,

which were well improved, were tenderly and assiduously devoted to their welfare, whether they were employed in the care of their health, their morals, or their religious improvement. Respecting the latter, she set them an excellent, pious example, faithfully attending religious meetings whenever her health permitted, and the exercise of her spirit therein was evident to those around her. Her care in engaging in the concerns of the church was remarkably guarded and very exemplary. In a word, she was a lovely companion and a sweet bosom friend, and it might be truly said of her that "she never made an enemy nor ever lost a friend, and to know her once was to love her forever."'

"She was buried in Friends' graveyard at West Chester."

From the numerous letters of sympathy received soon after his sad loss by the deeply sorrowing survivor we select as follows :

From George Dillwyn.

"BURLINGTON, Ninth month 20th, 1805.

"DEAR FRIEND,—I have just received thy son Thomas's letter of the 15th instant, which, as it was penned by thy desire, I consider as coming from thyself. I had previously thought of writing to thee on the affecting event to which it relates, and of which I was informed last evening, though I am sensible that on such occasions our sympathy with each other is more easily felt than expressed ; and that it is only in filial submission to the Divine will, that effectual relief and consolation are to be found. In addressing thee therefore, I had not so much in view the expression of my thoughts, as to mention the effect which the tidings had on my feelings. I have often noticed that such intelligence has been preceded by an uncommon depression of mind ; and so it was with me yesterday afternoon, when, thinking a little walk might help to cheer me, I called at my sister Moore's. To her I mentioned (perhaps in excuse for my dullness) the heaviness of my heart, which continued without intermission in the evening, when Mary Newbold joining us, brought in the account. Such intelligence, we might naturally suppose, was more likely to increase than abate sorrow; but truly it proved like rolling a stone from a well's mouth ; a tendering joy arose, and settled in a quieting, clear persuasion, (which still continues) that all is well, and forever well with dear *Rachel Collins*.

"After having imparted this, what can I add that will be worthy of thy attention? Let me, however, remind thee, that thou and thy R. C. have been permitted to travel through the greater part of life's wearisome pilgrimage together, and been favoured to surmount many dangers and difficulties, under which not a few of your contemporaries have failed. What though she has reached the object of your aim a little before thee,—your separation will not be long. She has not left thee alone, but surrounded with pleasant companions in the way, such as are studious, I trust, of thy comfort, and disposed to supply the void which this event has occasioned, by every means in their power.

"Martha Allinson and her family, desire the expression of their love may be added to my S. D.'s and mine; and with desires for thine and the dear children's support under the present and every other dispensation of unerring wisdom,

"I remain thy affectionate and sympathizing friend

"George Dillwyn.

"To Isaac Collins."

From James Ewing.

"Trenton, September 29th, 1805.

"Dear Sir,—I received early information of the irreparable loss which you have sustained, and should have been more prompt in noticing it, had my address been designed as one of mere complimentary condolence.

"Believe me, I participate so feelingly with you in your late bereavement, that I cannot believe a letter written or received during the first impassioned moments, could be as grateful, as when sober reason has recovered her seat.

"For me to say anything of the estimation in which your late partner was held, would be superfluous; her merits were duly appreciated by all her acquaintance, and are written in strong characters in the breasts of all those she honoured with her friendship. To have been the bosom companion of such a woman, is no trifling blessing; to have her removed from that situation, is an inexpressible loss. But you are to remember, that she was taken from you by the very hand who gave her; that very hand of Providence who gave her to be a blessing to you, who spared her so long to be a blessing to your family, has now thought proper to take her to Himself, undoubtedly in kindness to her, and probably to you likewise, perhaps to wean you from earth and earthly things, and to prepare you to follow her to that state of happiness which she now experiences. And is her death premature? By no means; though she has not lived to extreme old age, yet she has lived a long and useful life. Have you not greater reasons to adore the hand of Providence, who has lent her so long to you and yours, than to repine at her removal? I have no doubt your imagination is very fertile, in discovering the future plans of enjoyment and happiness which you might have had together, and that you frequently anticipate the pleasure you had in prospect and the delights of social converse which you promised yourself, of all which you are now bereft, and that under these recollections you are ready to cry out with good old Jacob, 'All these things are against me.'

"The ways of Providence are dark and intricate; perhaps she has been snatched away from evils to come, from distresses which we cannot foresee; at all events, would it not be better to turn your eyes back on the past, to recollect the tender anxiety she has felt for you in seasons of distress and difficulty, to recollect the great attentions she has paid to your family, the almost unparalleled prudence with which she has nursed them, raised them, educated and instructed them; can you not recollect that she has been spared to you until, under her hand, your numerous offspring have been reared almost to maturity; and can you not see in all this, the hand of an indulgent Providence? Methinks you might forget your sorrows for a moment, and dwell on recollections of this kind, until you could cry out with Job, in a kind of emphatical ecstasy, 'The Lord hath given, and the Lord hath taken away, blessed be the name of the Lord.'

"'Man is born to trouble, as the sparks fly upward.' You cannot expect to be exempt from the common lot of humanity; you have experienced perhaps as few of the ills of life as most men of your years; you have perhaps as many of the enjoyments of life remaining as most men; you have at least a competent share of this world's goods, you have many affectionate and agreeable friends; above all, you have a large and very promising family, none more so within the extent of my acquaintance; with these you can enjoy the remainder of your days. Be not then cast down, be not depressed under one misfortune, although the greatest; but bear up like a man and a Christian, always recollecting that you may shortly go to her, but that she can never return to you. I should be happy to hear from you and the family, and hope you will believe me to be, as ever,

"Your sincere friend

"JAMES EWING.

"TO ISAAC COLLINS."

*From Archibald Bartram.**

"PHILADELPHIA, October 31st 1805.

"MY DEAR UNCLE,—Though I have been hitherto silent, it was not the silence of unconcern. In secret I have mourned with thee, and our tears have been, as it were, mingled together. Alas! in the object of thy deep regret, have I not also suffered loss? There was a time when she was to me as a mother. I remember her offices of kindness, uniformly tendered, her salutary counsels, and her watchful concern for my welfare in sickness and in health. I think on these, and weep that she is to walk among us no more.

"Dear to me by the kindred tie, but drawn still closer by the bond of affliction, it is my desire to address thee in the language of consolation. To this my heart prompted me as soon as intelligence of the distressing event had reached my ears. I consulted my pillow; I asked counsel of the night; but could find no argument for consolation. Sad remembrance told me that there is a moment of anguish, when the voice of soothing strikes like discord on the ear, and the mind abhors the idea of drawing comfort from any consideration of time or sense. In such a moment, in answer to the officiousness of friendship, the agonized soul cries out, 'Let me alone, I will go down to the tomb, I will rest in the grave of my beloved.' But the mellowing influence of time will do much. When the tempest is gone over, and the whirlwind of conflicting passions has passed by, the still small voice of resignation is heard, and religion is ever ready to pour the wine and oil into the wounds of the virtuous breast; but of this thou knowest more than I can offer.

"Now that sorrow has subsided into a holy calm, I trust my dear uncle finds a melancholy satisfaction in recounting the virtues, and

* A nephew who had resided seven years in Isaac Collins's family.

dwelling on the amiable endowments of her whom he hopes to meet again in another and a better world. May we not extract reflections pensively pleasing, even from the fountain of our grief? Does not its poignancy afford an evidence that the virtuous attachments formed here, bidding defiance to the arrows of death, shall glow still stronger in another state? The chain of affection, stretched, but not broken, by the flight of a beloved object, seems to draw the fond soul up towards its counterpart, and heaven itself has superior attractions, when we are confident it is the dwelling-place of those so well beloved. Are such reflections wrong? I own they are not the result of reasoning, but they agree with my wishes and feelings. I know not if they are sanctioned by the wise, but I would not give them up for all the dictums of casuists or accuracy of logic. To me they have been a source of unspeakable consolation, buoying up my sinking soul above many a conflicting wave, and a confidence in their truth has ever awakened a more lively sense of the goodness of the bountiful Father of our being, who permits us to be cheered by such endearing hopes.

"Affection would urge me to write on. I could dwell with pleasure on many traits in the character of my excellent aunt, for on my heart they have made a lasting impression, but prudence forbids me to dwell too long upon the harrowing theme. Conversant in afliction's thorny path, and often a weary wanderer there, I can well understand the language of thy sorrows, and deeply sympathize in thy grief. That the universal Father will shelter us all under the wing of His love, is the ardent desire and constant hope of

"Thy affectionate nephew

"A. BARTRAM.

"To ISAAC COLLINS.

"P. S.—Remember me with the tenderest regard to all my cousins and tell them in their trials I wish to take a brother's share."

From Moses Brown.

"PROVIDENCE, Twelfth month 20th, 1805.

"DEAR ISAAC,—I have several times felt much sympathy with thee in thy bereavement of thy dear companion, and have had revived the remembrance of her when I saw her in Trenton, sitting with her amiable family; and the nearness I then felt has been also revived as I have lain on my pillow. I hope and trust thou hast been supported under thy great loss. None know the trial like those who have experienced it; but, dear Isaac, there is that which makes even those hard trials easy, and that has and can sanctify them for good, by drawing our affections from our most beloved object here to Himself, by His life-giving presence, enabling us to say Thy will be done. Yet even here, the sympathy of our friends is acceptable; I therefore though late, and of course not so lively, express mine, which might have been better sooner done, to a brother beloved, and conclude thy and family's sympathising affectionate friend

"MOSES BROWN.

"TO ISAAC COLLINS."

From John Cox.

"OXMEAD, near Burlington, Twelfth month 26th, 1805.

"DEAR FRIEND,—I seem not easy to let William meet his affectionate father, without hearing from me the expression of tender sympathy, which has been often felt by me and my dear Ann, when looking toward thee. The notice of our friends, on trying occasions, and under afflicting dispensations, I know is grateful, and Divine Providence is pleased sometimes to bless them as the means of lightening the load; yet I know, and doubt not but my dear friend has also experienced, that we have our 'changes,' and that seasons occur, when there is no spring of consolation, but as He is pleased to open it, and then we taste, in resignation to His will, of that pure water, whereby the fainting heart is revived, and the immortal part strengthened. I fear to express much; and though I have not before attempted it, may not have felt the less for the omission. I desire however, that thy hold on the Lord's sufficiency and confidence, not only in His power, but His will to make *all things* work together for *good*, may be steadfast. Nature will have its share. He who formed us and 'remembers that we are dust,' permits it so to be. He also knows the extent of thy great deprivation, and that of thy dear and valuable offspring;—and thy weak and faint efforts for resignation to His all-wise dispensations.

"These efforts, dear Isaac, weak as they are in thy own estimation, are doubtless acceptable to Him; and He who is wise and gracious in all His own righteous purposes, will continue, I do believe, to meet thy approaches, and strengthen every good desire, because they are of His own begetting. My wife cordially unites with me in near love to thee and thy dear children; and may we all bear in perpetual remembrance, that He 'afflicts not willingly;' and try to believe that 'He doeth all things well.'

"Thy truly affectionate friend,

"JOHN COX.

"TO ISAAC COLLINS."

From Isaac Collins to Moses and Elizabeth Bartram.

"WESTFARMS, 12 miles from New York, 10 mo. 1, 1805.

"MY DEAR BROTHER AND SISTER BARTRAM,—My mind having been in so tried a situation since the loss of my dearly beloved Wife, that I have not before put pen to paper, except in writing her Character, and lending some assistance in drawing up the short enclosed account of her Sickness and Death, which I have apprehended, would be acceptable to you. We had no Suspicion of her Disorder being the yellow fever till near the Close, and the Doctor who was, as a Physician, her favorite, was, I believe as ignorant as ourselves. So mild a Case it is tho't seldom ever occurred. She appeared to suffer very little pain, and looked well all the time. The fear of Death what she dreaded exceedingly when well, was entirely taken away, but she lay generally very quiet and said very little to any of us—we could not think her ill—we were not willing to think her so, yet every Thing was done that kind attention could dictate. Margaret Clapp, Nancy Cheesman, Jane Morton,* and Betsey Ann Valentine, four excellent Women, were with us, lending their aid to the last—it is impossible we should have fallen in better Hands—but all would not save my beloved—she is gone forever—I feel ruined and wholly undone—she was so lovely—every Thing to me. She was indeed the Crown and Diadem of our Family.

"William who has a few days since paid us a visit, Geo. Dillwyn from whom we have had a letter, and several other friends have had clear prospects of her Spirit's being rec'd into the Bosom of her

* Jane Cummings was married to George Morton on February 23, 1785; the latter died at Philadelphia in 1799; his widow then went to West Farms. Samuel G. Morton, son of George and Jane Morton, married Rebecca Grellet Pearsall in 1827.

Saviour—& what shall we say more? My Trouble and my feelings are wholly indescribable. I crave your sympathy and your prayers.

"Rebecca who was but poorly and weak before she was called to our assistance, has been, by this sudden and unexpected stroke reduced to a very low State of both body and mind but is now we think a little better. She has been confined to her bed ever since her Mother's Decease, some days not up more than five minutes in the Day. Yesterday however she sat up about two hours, without any apparent Disorder except weakness. The rest of us thro' favor are well in health. The Opportunity by which this goes to the post-office being ready I am obliged to close—in the interim I remain Your affectionate Brother

"ISAAC COLLINS."

ELEGY ON THE DEATH OF RACHEL COLLINS.

(*An affectionate tribute to her mourning family.*)

Of human bliss the tenure how uncertain!
O'er the fair aspect of the opening day
The threatening tempest draws its gloomy curtain;
Thus joy a moment gleams, and fades away.

Hope spreads before us her delusive promise,
Her fairy prospects glitter in our sight,
But sad remembrance drives the phantom from us,
And baffles all our projects of delight.

The friendships, fondly deemed to last forever
By ardent fancy, or the unpractised mind,
Opposing interests, adverse fortunes, sever:
A lasting friend, ah! where shall mortals find?

When mingling virtues dignify affection,
And wisdom owns the sentiment as just,
Death steps between, dissolves the dear connection,
And levels all our glories with the dust.

Life, I have found thee as a sea of trouble,
Whose fretful billows never are at rest;
And happiness as but a bursting bubble,
A twilight, a meteor's glare at best.

Thus mourned my spirit, when the griefs betiding
  Your much-loved circle reached my 'stonished ear;
Each earth-born wish, each earth bound prospect chiding,
  The warning cried, there's no continuance here.

From unsuspecting health, how soon was ravished
  The wife beloved, the parent ever kind!
On whom her rich endowments nature lavished—
  A beauteous form—a scarcely equalled mind.

Dear Anna, could the zeal of friendship borrow
  The shield of fate, its object to defend;
Could human skill avert the floods of sorrow,
  Thou hadst not lost a mother, I a friend.

But unavailing, when the summon's given,
  Are all the tears affection ever gave;
The sainted spirit wings its way to heaven,
  Nor heeds the sighings echoed round the grave.

Yet who can blame the filial love that hovers
  With pious fondness round that spot of earth,
And consecrates the mouldering dust that covers
  The precious relics of departed worth?

For not in vain were such attainments given:
  The heart they soften and the sense refine;
And sensibility, the child of heaven,
  Makes poor humanity almost divine.

Ye weeping sisters, often I behold you;
  In fancy's eye your pensive wanderings trace;
And with a brother's love would fain enfold you,
  And mingle sympathies with each embrace.

With you of all the long-drawn past conversing,
  Of seasons when our pastimes were the same;
With you, dear girls, a mother's praise rehearsing,
  I'd tell the virtues that enshrine her name.

Oft I beheld her, 'mid her infants thronging,
  The kind indulgence of a parent prove;
And oft impress the services belonging
  To one another and to heaven above.

With her we spent the Sabbath eve in reading
  The sacred records of the men of God,
Who from the pleasure of the world receding,
  Through thorny paths the way to glory trod.

How oft she warned us of the sly seductions,
  Like meshes spread, to ensnare unguarded youth!
How beauteous seemed, beneath her blest instructions,
  Religion's graces and the charms of Truth!

Mature her judgment was among the aged,
  Her piety the Christian did approve;
Her cheerful ease our younger hearts engaged—
  A link she seemed in heaven's great chain of love.

No narrow bounds her liberal soul confining,
  She followed Him who gave His life for all—
To guilt repentant, want, or sorrow pining,
  She gave relief, or wept at pity's call.

For life's poor veteran, 'neath misfortune drooping,
  Her faithful hand the cordial meal prepared;
The poor misguided wretch, to folly stooping,
  At once her bounty and her counsel shared.

Great were her virtues, happy was the dwelling
  Cheered by her smiles, enlightened by her lore.
How changed the scene! with sighs each bosom swelling,
  We long shall mourn—she walks with us no more.

But thou, with folded arms and tears fast flowing,
  What mind to suffering bent thy griefs could weigh,
When, 'neath the mighty stroke of judgment bowing,
  Thy crown and diadem were ta'en away?

Had I the gift of eloquent persuasion,
  Were mine the son of Jesse's soothing art,
With kindred zeal I'd seek the blest occasion
  To heal thy wounds and bind thy broken heart.

But He who keeps the master-key of feeling
  Inspires with joy or chastens us with pain;
The gracious God alone, His will revealing,
  Can tune thy soul to harmony again.

By His blest aid, each adverse will subduing,
  "Lord, as thou wilt," be our resignèd strain;
In clouds of darkness He is watchful viewing
  The patient soul, and light shall beam again.

1806. A. BARTRAM.

Extract from a Letter by George Dillwyn.

"BURLINGTON, First month 28th, 1806.

"I note thy prospect of retiring from business; and if thy partiality for Jersey should prove a means of thy being readded to our little company here, before we are detached from it, I believe it will be a pleasing circumstance to all, but to none more than to my S. D. and Thy affectionate friend,

"GEORGE DILLWYN.

"TO ISAAC COLLINS."

In 1808, Seventh month 8, Isaac Collins purchased a house for four thousand dollars, in Burlington, at the northeast corner of York and Broad Streets, with an adjoining lot of one and a half acres. This property remained in the family till 1871. The house is probably at this date (1893) one hundred years old.

On the 9th of Tenth month, 1809, Isaac Collins married Deborah Smith, widow of Benjamin Smith, and daughter of the venerable and much-beloved Margaret Morris. Her two children were Daniel B. and Mar-

RESIDENCE OF ISAAC COLLINS, BURLINGTON, N. J.

garet Morris Smith,* the former known for many years as the senior partner of the firm of Smith & Hodgson, at the northeast corner of Sixth and Arch Streets, Philadelphia. Afterwards he became Professor of Moral and Intellectual Philosophy at Haverford, in 1833, being greatly esteemed by the students for his urbanity of manner, sound views of morality and religion, and rare facility in imparting knowledge.

In the quiet old town of Burlington Isaac Collins enjoyed the society of many of his earlier friends. Still retaining his love of agriculture and horticulture, he planted in his garden choice fruit-trees of various kinds, the product of which his great-grandchildren enjoyed many a time. A few acres out of town supplied grazing and food for a horse, which was often used in visiting his friends and neighbors within a few miles of Burlington.

The old meeting-house where from 1770 to 1777 he had met with others in religious worship had been taken down, and the one now standing (1893) had been built on the site. Under one of the two large buttonwood-trees noticeable in the rear of the old hexagonal meeting-house an Indian chief, it is said, pitched his wigwam in very early times. A tree of the same kind, in Green Bank, on the river front, is very probably of the same age, as it is the one to which was made fast the

---

* Margaret Morris Smith spent the greater part of her life in Burlington, in a house on Main Street, a few doors below Broad Street, where she entertained her friends in true Christian hospitality. She was also noted for her sympathy with and generous aid to the poor or the unfortunate, and her life was eventually sacrificed in efforts for their relief, more especially on the occasion of a terrible railway accident, from which several of the sufferers were taken in and nursed at her house.

cable of the good ship Shields, which landed a company of Quakers in 1678.

While thus so pleasantly retired from the cares of business, surrounded by affectionate friends and relatives, and cheered by frequent visits of his children, Isaac Collins was attacked with a painful malady which often deprived him of social intercourse and put his fortitude to the severest test. Unaccustomed to sickness during the greater part of his former life, his sufferings pressed the more heavily upon him, and in the course of a few years his constitution, originally one of great firmness, was worn down, and he was reduced to a state of great weakness and exhaustion. A short time before the opening of the spring in 1817, a slight paralytic affection indicated a critical state of his health, and a few weeks after this attack the violence of the disease rapidly increased and wasted away his already enfeebled body.

On the 21st of Third month, 1817, after several weeks of great suffering, which he bore with Christian patience, he peacefully passed away in the seventy-second year of his age.

Extract from a Letter by Sarah Collins, dated 1817.

"My beloved parent continued growing weaker and weaker till the 21st inst., when he departed this life in peace, the grave having no terrors nor death any sting. His interment took place on the 25th, and was a season solemnized to many.

"He was in his 72nd year. Eleven of his children and five of his children-in-law followed him to the grave. His closing scene was calm, and a full possession of the mental faculties permitted. We were enabled, through divine assistance, to resign our dearly beloved and highly valued parent, at the awful moment of dissolution, without a murmur. We remained, according to his wish, in silence around the bed nearly an hour after the spirit had left its tenement of clay, and the body also, agreeably to his wish, remained some hours unmoved. Dear George Dillwyn, with many other friends, called in next morning, deeply sympathizing with us in our close trial."

He was buried in Friends' graveyard in Burlington, and a plain stone, inscribed only with his name and dates of birth and death, marks the spot.

There were several well-recognized traits in the character of Isaac Collins. Of these may briefly be mentioned his strict veracity and integrity in business, as a proof of which it is deserving of particular notice that when purchasing goods on credit, they were sold to him on his simple verbal promise of payment at the time stipulated, he having never given his note in payment. The usual practice of endeavoring to buy goods at the lowest possible rates was his aversion, as he was unwilling to rob the industrious mechanic or honest tradesman of his just rights. It was a rule with him also, in dealing with persons of moderate circumstances, either to pay cash or to solicit early bills for labor or goods ordered by him. The same sense of justice led him to manumit, while living in Trenton, his slave George, who had served him faithfully a number of years, and to make provision for his support in after-life. At that time slavery was allowed and recognized by the Society of Friends.

Knowing the great advantages of a good education, he was a very active promoter and manager of public and private schools, while his sympathy for the sick or afflicted induced him to take an interest in the management of the City Hospital in New York, of which he was for some years one of the governors.

His contributions to objects of distress as well as to

benevolent institutions were liberal in proportion to his means, yet regulated by a discriminating judgment which forbade his furnishing the vicious or profligate with the means for continuing their former career.

It may be mentioned as an evidence of his good judgment that in his last will he left more to his daughters than to his sons, judging that the latter could more easily provide for themselves.

During his residence in Trenton, and after his removal to New York, his house was ever open to receive his friends, especially those who were travelling ministers, whose company he esteemed a privilege, and considered it an advantage to his young family.

He had the highest veneration for the Holy Scriptures, and it was his daily custom to read portions of them to his assembled family. The system planned on the continent of Europe, a short time previous to the French Revolution, for the annihilation of civil society, morality, and religion, filled his mind (at times) with fear and horror.

It was a cause of great satisfaction to him in his latter years that he had never published any works detrimental to the moral or religious education of the community, and that he had instilled such a principle in those of his sons who succeeded him in the printing and publishing business.

LETTERS.

"New York, 11mo 4th, 1796.

"My dear Sister,—Thy very acceptable letter was handed to Charles by a young Man he did not know, but probably it was Betsey Cassel's Husband as I was informed she was the bearer—if I knew where to find her I would go to see her, as it no doubt would be very agreeable to her to be noticed by a relation that has lived in Philad[a].

"The little Handkerchiefs by Molly Clark came safe and I request that thee will enquire of brother Joseph if he has any money of ours in his hands—if I paid him for Almanacks or anything else—if he had, I wish him to pay thee for the Handkerchiefs and charge them to Isaac Collins as he is, I believe, the only person in Phila[da] that we have an open account with. Brother Moses owes me a little rosewater for the last salted roses I sent him which I request may be sent when the dried peaches arrive from Harrisburg and are forwarded to New York by water.

"It was indeed a favor to move our little ones so great a distance, without any injury or accident but were exceedingly disappointed in not receiving our goods and printing office that was sent round by Phila[da] in a day or two after we got here: instead of that, it was seventeen days from the time the vessel set off before she arrived at this port—thee may imagine how very anxious we were and fearfull she had foundered at sea; however she came at last without any damage, to the joy of the whole family and I hope a degree of thankfulness to Him who rules the stormy ocean and at His command the raging sea is still.

"Our dear little Mary and Joseph have been most cruelly treated by the musketoes. Mary was recovering when I got there, but poor Joseph was attacked the first night and in a few days he looked as if he had the small pox very bad—he scratched the bites and they festered and inflamed so much that he could get little sleep and had it continued I question whether he would have survived many more bites, but, at this time he is better and looks an altered child, is bravely as to health except a cough, yet that is so like it I doubt it to be the Whooping Cough.

"Poor Becky Christie, how long and painful are her complaints—she has had a trying life since her marriage, but if they are so to her, she will have reason at the close, to thank the Lord, and such an acknowledgment I have heard her make in a letter to a friend that it was permitted for her good and no more than she deserved—if she is taken, her poor little nephews will lose a good friend that I fear cannot be replaced.

"Do, my dear, prevail on thyself to keep up a correspondence with me as thro' thee I wish and expect to hear from my friends in Phila[da] particularly, which will be to me very grateful, especially now, as I live at so great a distance from it. Tell Brother Joseph and Benjamin that I wish them not to forget that they have a sister in New York that would be pleased to hear from them by letters from each or either—give my love to all and accept a large portion for thyself and beloved family from thy affectionate

"RACHEL COLLINS."

Endorsed,

"MOSES BARTRAM, Druggist,
"No. 58 North Second Street, Phila[da]."

"NEW YORK, 9 mo. 2[d], 1800.

"MY DEAR MARY,—Thy letter of the 29 of last month came safe to hand and I am thankful that you are all favoured with health, and pleased that thee is engaged in making a sampler which I desire thee will execute with great neatness and accuracy as a specimen of the needle work of the boarding school.* We have written some letters since the return of our beloved friend Hannah Clement and thy sister, but thro' omission they have not been sent—friend Clement is still in this city but expects to go to Monthly meeting at Flushing to-morrow—they are both in their usual health—thy sisters Sarah and Ann with Robert and Betsey at Flushing who have taken part of an house for the benefit of dear little Robert's health which is rather delicate, but better than it has been. Charles is in Phila[da] on business so that we have quite a small family. Thomas and Susan are gone this afternoon in company with some young people from Burlington and expect to return in the evening—this large and populous city continues to be preserved from any contagious disease and in general very healthy—not a single case of the yellow fever is believed to be here which is cause of thankfulness to the Almighty dispenser of every good—tell thy brother Isaac not to be discouraged from writing because Tommy has not answered his letter, for he is a good deal engaged in the printing office—we are printing Lindley Murray's large grammar which will be finished and ready for sale in

* Nine Partners.

a few weeks—give my love to Anny Merriet and Esther Hallet in particular and the whole valuable household in general.

"I am thy affectionate Mother,

"RACHEL COLLINS."

"NEW YORK 11 mo. 6, 1806.

"MY DEAR NEPHEW ARCH^D^ BARTRAM,—I duly received thy very affecting and sympathetic Letter of the 31st of 10th month and should have been more prompt in replying to it, had we not been on the Point of returning to our mournful habitation after an absence of nearly two months, and since which we have been unavoidably taken up in the line of our business—

"My great—my sore Bereavement is still very heavy upon me, and when it will feel less so, I do not know. I tho't I had suffered much in sympathy with my son Charles in the course of the last year, in the loss of full thirty thousand dollars by bad Debts, and in his failure in consequence of it. But alas! I knew nothing what suffering was. I had then no Experience of what I have since suffered, nor could I feel fully for another's woe, without that Experience. The Loss of all my property, or even that of my Children, dear as they are would not have been equal to the Loss of my beloved, the cheerful, the accomplished, the faithful friend of my bosom. O! how I miss her on so many occasions—her company—her counsel—her affection—her caresses. She indeed in my Eyes and I believe, in those of many others, was altogether lovely. Having her, I wanted few if any other companions. But it is said, the meliorating hand of Time will blunt the keenest edge—it may be so, but of this I have had no experience. She was indeed the Crown and Diadem of our family, and equal at all times for what was called for at her hands. But I trust and hope that her virtuous attachments formed here and sanctioned by heaven itself, bidding defiance to the arrows of Death, will glow still stronger in another and a better world. Here, my dear Archy, is a new, an additional Incitement so to live and so to act as to be enabled thro' the divine favor to join them in the mansions of peace and Joy where Sorrow never enters. That this may be our happy Lot is the ardent desire of my heart.

"Besides thine, we have received many other excellent letters of sympathy and Condolence from some of the best of friends, and they indeed feel at times like so many Cordials to our drooping and sorrowing minds, all evincing the high esteem in which my precious Rachel was held.

"We are getting forward with the Bible, being almost through first Chronicles and now have two Presses running pretty steadily on it. But Business to me is no longer any pleasure, nor have I much inducement to continue at it longer than will be sufficient to complete this work. I have pretty much made up my mind to retire into the country to a quiet Habitation and there mourn out the remainder of my days which may not be many.

"It would gratify us—it would console us if some of our dear Relatives would come and pay us a visit and none more so than thyself. Cousin Sarah Lippincott loved thy dear aunt much—we could wish her to come with thee, being like her as to cheerfulness and otherwise of a similar Disposition, so I have conceived her to be.

"Ever since my precious R's decease, I seem to have felt a double portion of Love and Respect for her Relatives and Connections. I want to see many of them face to face, but my Business, were there nothing else in the way, will not permit me to leave Home, perhaps till the Bible is finished.

"Our love flows to every Branch of the family and particularly so at this time to all under thy dear father and Mother's roof while I subscribe as ever

"thy affectionate Uncle
"ISAAC COLLINS."

"BURLINGTON 5 mo. 12, 1808.

"MY DEAR SARAH,*—Strange as the Thing may seem to be to some and extraordinary to others I am really living in B, and which is a quiet Habitation. I am pleased with the premises I occupy, My Peas are in Blossom, Carrots, Beets and Parsnips are up—Sallad of divers kinds on the Table when we please. Potatoes are also up, and I have planted various kinds of Pole, Dwarf and Lima Beans, and I have gotten some Cabbage plants set out. We have a very great show of Strawberries, Raspberries, Currants, Plums, and some Gooseberries, several small Cherry trees full of fruit. We have been too much engaged about many Things: There is so much to do that

* His daughter.

by Night every Day we go to bed weary—sleep some—rise betimes and at it again.

"Geo. Dillwyn, Jno. Cox, Rebecca Archer and Sarah Hull who is on the way to the Y. M. have all blowed the Gospel Horn, since our arrival here as well as several others of less Notoriety, so that, if we do not improve, it will be our own faults. This would be a delightful place for Stephen & Rebecca, if they could feel it so. She would improve in her Health—there being plenty of Physicians for Soul & Body. Thee & Susan I believe must take turn about in keeping house for the Boys so that each of you may partake of the sweets of the delightful Spot. I shall long to see all my Children & Grandchildren here by turns and their passing back & forward will contribute to their health. Betsy must come & visit the place of her Nativity and bring as many of her Babes as she please but little *Rebec* must be one—she is so sweet a cherub—kiss her for me.

"We have had a very heavy storm I hope William has not set out previous thereto by water on his Southern Expedition. Thomas is at Phila[da]—he has been very little with us since we came. I wish he was well settled with a good wife. It is likely he will return to-morrow and on 2d day start for Home. He must be much wanted in the office.

"I have just come from Market, excellent Butter for 15d—veal, 6d for a nice Leg or Loin & Eggs 13d per score—Rebecca Archer expects to attend the Y. M. I want thee & Susan to make her acquaintance. I have none—She is an elegant Preacher.

"Give my love to every individual of my children—young & old—and accept the same from

"Thy affec[te] father
"ISAAC COLLINS."

To his Wife Deborah.

"BURLINGTON 4 mo. 16, 1811.

"MY DEAR,—This is the 3rd day since thou left us. It was a dreary day. Meeting both fore and afternoon was dull enough, but in the evening Joseph and myself tea'd at Sister Willis' where Brother Morris spent part of the time. Second-day Morn; Margaret M. and I took a ride to Joseph Smith's, spent an agreeable Hour and returned via the Sluice Bank. In the afternoon Sister W. went with me to Green Hill where we found all well, and after wandering about the Garden and other parts of those delightful Grounds and talking about planting a few pink Roots which we took with us and pruning some Shrubs we met with about the Garden fence, complimenting Mame Biles about her Beaux lately there on a visit, having spent an hour or so, we set off Home. We however just rode up to John Cox's to inquire if all were well, which Becca answering in the affirmative and after strolling about his very handsome Gardens, we made the best of our Way to the Retreat and a delightful Spot it is. In the Evening we met again at dear Mother's who is still a little poorly—the Effects of a Cold—where we took Tea—after which I returned to the Retreat to rest being not a little fatigued. But I am preparing for my Wilmington Jaunt, and therefore I have rode nine Miles to day, taking Sally Sharpless with me. She came in from West Hill last evening when all were well—all these circumstances, I mention that thou, my dear, may report to the several parties concerned, as it may fall in thy way—What delightful weather you have for the meeting! I hope the Body of friends may be edified and bring something good Home to dispense among their *poor* friends and neighbors.

"I am to have a party to tea—the particulars in my next. Joseph is at work in the Garden, but I have attended my Wife's advice in taking care of her Husband. I hope Robert Boune, daughter, cousin and friend & Jno. Murray will call and see me on their Return & dear Charles without fail. Press them all.

"I hope to get a letter from thee to-morrow and tell me what is done with Jesse's prospect, if it be resulted.

"My love is to all enquiring friends, particularly my kindred—the ties of Nature,—Farewell, my dear and believe me to be as ever

"Thy affectionate
"ISAAC COLLINS."

To his Son Joseph.

"BURLINGTON 1 mo. 19, 1812.

"DEAR JOSEPH,—I have thy acceptable letter of the 5th by Thomas. I am happy to find thou art engaged in the store, and that you have Business pretty brisk. This is a particular favor at such a Time when so many thousands do not know how to turn themselves for a living. The events at Richmond,* I hope and trust will be a solemn warning to the youth of other Cities, and especially to the young Men and Women of our Society. Plays and Playhouses have been the Bane and Ruin of Thousands, as they sow the Seeds of every species of Vice and Immorality. I hope I have not a child that would be seen at one of them—it would disgrace them in the Eyes of all good Men. I am not a little mortified that one of our relatives has been indulging herself in this way since she has been in New York. I was sincerely glad she was at Home—Such are really not fit Company for Christians.

* * * * * * * * * * *

"I must leave the cause of the poor Spaniards to the great Disposer of Human Events. He it is that ruleth Nations by His Providence as do Princes their subjects. I believe it is a perfect mystery to Bonaparte why he is able to do thus and so. He no doubt is astonished at his own, as he supposes, doings. But he may yet become, as did Nebuchadnezzar, like the ox that licketh up the grass.

"I shall like to hear from thee when thou feels disposed to be in my Company in this way, and when leisure will permit.

"From thy affectionate father

"ISAAC COLLINS."

"TO JOSEPH B. COLLINS."

To Hannah Collins.

"BURLINGTON 1 mo. 19, 1812.

"MY BELOVED DAUGHTER,—I have thy affectionate little Letter which is particularly interesting as it portrays some of the charms of thy little Pet. Give her a kiss for each of her Burlington Grandparents, who are anxious to see her, when they could the better judge whether the little darling appeared to be all Collins.

"It is very grateful to my feelings that Joseph has been so graciously received among his friends at N. Y. The Business is that of *his choice*, and I hope after a while he will become quite reconciled to the disagreeable part of it. He has, I believe entered the Store with the best Intentions, and I am willing to hope will prove himself particularly useful there as well as agreeable to your domestic Circle.

---

* Burning of the theatre, when hundreds, unable to get out, lost their lives.

I wish Benjn to furnish him with whatever he may stand in need of, to save his clothes at my Expense, say an Apron and a sailors round-about Coat to do his work in &c.

"My D.C. unites in Love to all your fireside, not forgetting little Elisa—also to Brother & Sister Bowne.

"From thy affectionate father

"ISAAC COLLINS."

"BURLINGTON 10 mo. 25, 1814.

"MY DEAR DAUGHTER HANNAH COLLINS,—Understanding by a letter from dear Sarah that thou art in a delicate State of Health, we have thought a little Excursion to this place would perhaps be useful. We wish thou would try the Experiment—thy so doing would tend to reinstate thy Health, or at least improve it. In this case my son William will meet thee with my Horse & Chaise at any Time and place thou wilt please to appoint. It shall not cost thee one farthing either coming or returning, or if thou and Benny would prefer it, we should be glad you would both come and bring the Children and spend the winter with us. If you will come we will endeavor to make our peaceful Habitation as agreeable as we can.

"Be not cast down—I hope and trust you will yet see happier and more prosperous days. My sympathy has been called up on hearing of thy dear father's trouble and of that of the family Connection so that Tears have trickled down my cheeks. Trust in God—He is a sure Helper in the needful Time—I have found Him so. What shall I say more?

* * * * * * * * * * *

"Thy truly affectionate father

"ISAAC COLLINS.

"It has been mentioned, I believe by Thomas that G. Dillwyn may be accommodated with good quarters at No. 189 Pearl Street. If he should be disposed to accept the Invitation I have no doubt that every attention will be paid to make him feel at Home. He is really a prince in our Israel. I believe if Wm. & Benjamin would find him as much of their company as possible, they would not only be gratified but improved. He is fond of the Company of young people—is a man of much observation—full of anecdote and has travelled much in Europe and America."

BIOGRAPHIES.

BIOGRAPHIES.

REBECCA GRELLET, wife of Stephen Grellet, died in Burlington, New Jersey, Ninth month 3, 1861, in her eighty-ninth year.

In her early days she listened to her Saviour's invitation, "Seek ye my face," and responded to the call. Through the whole course of her life she steadily followed her Lord and Master. Humility, purity, and refinement were conspicuous traits in her character. To rare discretion and sound judgment she added a very uncommon degree of sympathy, which eminently qualified her to be a wise counsellor to those who sought her advice and consolation. In 1804 she was married to Stephen Grellet, the well-known and highly-honored French Quaker minister. A better idea cannot be given of the close and tender tie which united her beloved husband and herself than by quoting from his journal, dated Third month, 1831, when about to commence his fourth journey to Europe:

"My beloved wife, on this occasion as on all preceding ones, which have not been few since we became united together by the endearing tie of the marriage engagement, freely and with Christian cheerfulness, resigned me to the Lord's service. She is uniformly a great encourager to me to act the part of a faithful servant to the best of Masters. Her soul travails with mine in such a manner that she had been deeply sensible of the nature of the service that the great Master called me to, before I had disclosed to her or to any one the secret exercises of my heart."

She occupied acceptably for many years the important station of elder, and her service in this capacity was not suspended even during her seclusion as an invalid, those who resorted to her as to a mother in Israel being often made to drink from wells of spiritual refreshment, and the Gospel messengers whose visits she received with tender appreciation being in turn watered themselves. Her intellectual powers, which were of no common order, continued to be bright and vigorous till the end of Second month, 1861, when she was seized with paralysis, after which life gently ebbed away. Her countenance was beautifully peaceful in death, as if she were reposing on the bosom of Him who loved her, had redeemed her, and was leading her through the valley to the regions of light and eternal blessedness.

A memoir of the family and connections of Isaac and Rachel Collins would be incomplete without some information in regard to Stephen Grellet, so widely known in our country and on the continent of Europe as a true and faithful messenger of the Gospel.

Étienne de Grellet de Mabillier, better known by the name of Stephen Grellet, was born at Limoges, in France, on the 2d of Eleventh month, 1773. His parents, who were Roman Catholics, were nearly allied to the nobility. At a very early age he was susceptible to deep religious impressions and the efficacy of prayer. But afterwards, seeking after happiness in worldly amusement, and not finding it, he "wondered that the name of pleasure could be given to anything of the kind." Before he was sixteen his father's estates were confiscated, and he and his brothers entered the Royalist army, being enlisted in the King's Horse-Guards. Having been taken prisoners of war, he and his elder brother Joseph were ordered to be shot; but a sudden commotion occurring at the time of execution, they escaped and went to Amsterdam; thence they sailed for Demerara, arriving there in First month, 1793. A report being spread that the French were coming to take possession of the colony, they went to New York, and settled for a short time in Newtown, Long Island. At this period Stephen Grellet was nearly twenty-two years of age. Here his religious impressions were again awakened by what seemed an awful and audible voice proclaiming, "Eternity! Eternity!" Reading the Bible, earnest prayer, and attending the ministry of "Friends," resulted in his thorough conversion and dedication to the service of the Lord.

Going to Philadelphia in Twelfth month, 1795, he met with a very cordial reception, being offered an opportunity for a lucrative business, but he concluded to teach French for a living.

He spoke in the ministry for the first time on First month 20, 1796, and nine months afterwards was received into membership at the North Meeting on Sixth Street. In Third month, 1798, he was recorded as a minister of Jesus Christ.

For particulars respecting this eminent servant of the Lord the reader is referred to his biography, edited by Benjamin Seebohm, detailing not only his various missionary travels, exceeding in extent those of any other in his own Society, but also the deep exercises of his mind, preparatory to entering upon the visits to which the Holy Spirit directed him.

His polite and courteous manners aided him in access

to persons of every rank and condition in life, and the Lord was graciously pleased to grant him such unction and power as to make a deep and lasting impression upon kings, emperors, the nobility, the common people, convicts, and soldiers wherever his lot was cast.

It was not only in his public ministrations that his light shone brightly. He adorned the Gospel he preached by his meekness and patience, his Christian charity and brotherly kindness, his watchfulness and humility, his holy life and conversation.

After having for more than fifty years labored diligently in the service of his Master in various parts of the world, he attended the Yearly Meeting of Friends in Philadelphia in 1847, but was taken ill, and was obliged to return to his home in Burlington. From that time he did not leave it for a single night.

His last illness was short, but one of extreme suffering, which he bore without a murmur, and when the summons came his lamp was trimmed and burning, his work was finished, and he departed this life in the full hope and confidence of a blessed immortality. "Mark the perfect man, and behold the upright: for the end of that man is peace."

He died on the 16th of Eleventh month, 1855, aged eighty-two years, and was laid to rest in Friends' burial-ground in Burlington.

We append the following extract from the pen of one of his nephews, who enjoyed for years the acquaintance and the Christian counsel of the beloved relative:

"With one true friend thy lot was cast on Norway's rugged shore,
Where wintry storms among the pines in fearful concert roar,
Or Russia's steppes, a level waste, in lonely silence lie,
Uncheered by trace of human life or warm and genial sky.

Where flows the wide romantic Rhine, its hills and vales among,
Or lie the isles of classic Greece, the theme of Pagan song;
Or where proud Stamboul lifts her towers and minarets from the
sea,
And the muezzin's cry full oft is heard to bow in prayer the knee;
Where lived and died the faithful few in Smyrna's busy mart,
Or sculptured column still attests the famed Athenian's art,
Jew, Gentile, Pagan, crowding came, in mute and strange surprise,
To hear the solemn words of truth and mark thy simple guise.
Within the walls of ancient Rome 'twas given thee to bear
A mandate from the King of kings, unharmed, to despots there,
And, like the bold apostle once, the Nazarene proclaim,
None daring to forbid thee then to speak His wondrous name.
In court or camp—in humble life, or by an emperor's throne—
No flattery swerved thee from thy path, thy Maker to disown,
Nor threat of man could make thee pause, to coward fear a prey,
Or, for a moment, dim the light that shone around thy way.
To serf and noble, crafty priest or pontiff in his pride,
Was preached alike to one and all a Saviour crucified,
And humble Christians, by the world deserted or forgot,
In some vast city's solitude, or wild, secluded spot,
Gathered around in joy to hear the houseless wanderer tell
In accent strange of One they knew and honored well,
While grateful tones and hymns of praise rose on the desert air
In after-years that He had sent that welcome pilgrim there."

J. C.

Charles Collins, the eldest son of Isaac and Rachel Collins, was born First month 14, 1774. He was among the very few in the Society of Friends in New York who maintained their ancient testimony against the iniquitous system of slavery. For many years he kept a store for the exclusive sale of the products of free labor, and conscientiously refrained from the use in his family of the unrequited toil of the slave. The following anecdote, which I have often heard related, is characteristic of the man. Coming out of meeting when it was raining fast, a friend invited Charles to partake of the shelter offered by his umbrella, which he readily accepted; but they had proceeded only a short distance when, raising his eyes, he discovered that the umbrella was made of cotton. He instantly left his friend, preferring to walk in the rain to being sheltered by the product of slave labor.

He was sorely grieved at the retrograde movements of the Monthly Meeting in New York in relation to the righteous testimony against this "sum of all villanies," and often remonstrated with divers individuals on the subject. Finding his earnest entreaties unavailing, he finally concluded to withdraw from membership, and a short time before his decease he prepared a paper of resignation and sent it to a member, to be presented to the meeting; but we are informed that his request was not complied with.

Charles Collins was emphatically the friend of the oppressed, regardless of nation, complexion, or sect; and perhaps there are few, if any, who so entirely overcame every feeling of resentment. If he apprehended any individual had aught against him or any other friend, he would immediately call upon the person and endeavor to have the cause of dissatisfaction removed.

To the above may be added the following anecdote respecting him. He once invited the writer, a nephew, then on a visit in New York, to go with him to the office of the Anti-Slavery Society. Purchasing a few tracts, and having them in a package ready to be tied up, he said to the clerk, "Where did that cotton string come from?" "From the South," was the reply. "Leave it off. I don't use such strings!" was the emphatic remark of Charles Collins. J. C.

Sarah Collins, the second daughter of Isaac and Rachel Collins, was born Sixth month 2, 1775; married Nathaniel Hawxhurst, Seventh month 13, 1826; and died Fourth month 23, 1855, nearly eighty years of age.

From the Friends' Review, Fifth month 19, 1855.

"Died at her residence in the city of New York on the 23d of Fourth month, 1855, Sarah C. Hawxhurst, an esteemed minister of the Society of Friends. From her youth she had been devoted to the promotion of truth and righteousness and the welfare of suffering humanity, irrespective of color, country, or creed. Distrustful of herself, yet firm in adhering to what she believed to be her duty, she desired to follow peace with all men, and with remarkable simplicity of character, filled up her appointed sphere of labor,—'diligent in business, fervent in spirit, serving the Lord.' She devoted much time and personal service to the various charitable institutions in New York, in which she felt a lively interest; but her chief object was the circulation and promoting the reading of the Holy Scriptures and religious tracts. She was ever watching for suitable opportunities to distribute them, and probably circulated hundreds of thousands of pages during her life. It may be said of her that she 'loved mercy, did justly, and walked humbly with her God,' and her friends have the consoling assurance that through redeeming mercy she has entered into the joy of her Lord."

From the Advocate and Guardian, New York, Sixth month 1, 1857.

"At the afternoon session the following resolution was offered:

"'WHEREAS, We have occasion to recognize the admonitory voice of Divine Providence in the death of Mrs. Sarah C. Hawxhurst, a beloved sister, whose pleasant smile has so often greeted us at our annual gatherings, and whose faithful labors terminated but with life.

"'*Resolved*, That we will cherish the affectionate remembrance of her lovely example, praying that it may long exert a hallowed influence upon survivors, and induce many to follow her as she followed Christ.'"

From the same Institution.

"The managers of the Society, in presenting their twenty-first annual report, have occasion to record the death of one of their oldest and most highly esteemed vice-presidents. In the providence that has removed Mrs. Sarah C. Hawxhurst from the cares of earth to the joys of heaven, this Society, in common with others that have long enjoyed her valuable services, has sustained a loss that will be deeply felt. Her presence at its annual gatherings for the past eighteen years, her gentle, loving spirit, her efforts to do good as she had opportunity, the savor of her excellent example and faithful testimony, will be held sacred in the remembrance of all who were privileged to listen to her words of wisdom.

"May her frequent exhortations to youthful Christians to prepare to take the places of those who are passing away, be heeded now as a voice from the grave. She has gone hence at the advanced age of fourscore years 'as a shock of corn cometh in in his season.'"

Extract from a letter written in St. Louis by the President of the Society, who was seeking improvement in health in a far-distant State.

"And now would that I could take my seat beside you, at the Annual Meeting, in the midst of well-remembered faces, some of whom we meet only on these occasions, others whom we have long loved and with whom we have long labored, but 'one is not,' for God has taken her, even in the brief space since we parted. Yes, that dear, kind face, those lips that never parted but to utter the words of heavenly wisdom, the words that never wounded overburdened hearts, but cheered and pointed heavenward, are to greet us here no more. She has seemed for years to stand on the edge of Jordan, and now she has passed over. A peaceful exit, I have no doubt, though I have not heard the particulars. I need not call her name. One of the earliest and warmest friends of our Society, who died a martyr to the cause, asserted that she never flattered, never hesitated in her work—the work of her Master—of whatever kind. She was 'gentle, pure, peaceable, easily entreated,' not thinking of herself more highly than she ought to think—full of good works.

"Where can I stop? For of none could it be said more truly,

she was a vessel meet for her Master's service, a temple for the Holy Ghost to dwell in. May her meek and heavenly spirit long abide in our midst.

"I received a note from her addressed to our board meeting in April, but it came too late to be read. It contained an exhortation to be more diligent in work and fervent in spirit.

"May 1, 1855."

Elizabeth Collins, the fourth child of Isaac and Rachel Collins, was born on the 23d of Seventh month, 1776, in Burlington, New Jersey, where her parents resided until 1778. In her thirteenth year she was one of the girls, arrayed in white dresses, who sang an ode of welcome, as George Washington, President-elect, was crossing the Assanpink bridge, in Trenton, on his way to New York to be inaugurated. It was a memorable occasion, as they strewed flowers before him in the presence of matrons of the best families in that city. The note of acknowledgment by Washington is still preserved, expressive of his deep emotion and gratitude at this mark of public esteem.

In her twenty-first year she married Robert Pearsall, of Long Island, and after the marriage of their eldest daughter Rachel to John Jay Smith, they removed to Philadelphia.

While still young much of the care of the ten brothers and sisters still younger devolved upon herself, thereby aiding her mother in all her domestic duties.

She was of short stature, brunette complexion, and dark eyes, bearing, it is said, more resemblance to her mother than any other member of the family.

She died at the age of eighty-one years, in Germantown, where she had resided a long time.

Thomas Collins, the second son of Isaac and Rachel Collins, was born in Trenton, New Jersey, Third month 3, 1779, and died in Burlington, First month 22, 1859, in the eightieth year of his age. He was early trained in the printing-office of his father, becoming an excellent proof-reader and a steady workman at the old-fashioned lever press. When of suitable age he was taken into partnership, the duties of which he faithfully fulfilled, finding also time to attend to some public business. He became a life member of the American Bible Society, the Manumission Society, etc. In the management of public schools he also took part. In 1812 he married Ann Abbott, daughter of John and Susan Abbott, of Abbottsville, a few miles south of Trenton, and having accumulated what he believed to be sufficient to support his family, he removed, in 1818, with his wife and three children to Burlington, New Jersey, residing in the house, at the northeast corner of York and Broad Streets, that had been occupied by his father from 1808 to 1817. Here he led a quiet life for more than forty years. He took great pleasure in cultivating the tract of land belonging to the property, and more particularly in improved methods of gardening and the raising of fine fruit. As his sons grew up he gave all of them the advantage of a liberal education. Several of them attended Haverford School, the eldest becoming a teacher, which profession he continued for more than twenty-five years.

Though of a retiring disposition, not seeking publicity, he greatly enjoyed the society of his relatives and friends, and more especially that of ministers of the Gospel. To them and to the members of Burlington Quarterly Meeting his house was always open.

FROM LIFE, BY [illegible]

THOMAS COLLINS.

His sympathies were very much in favor of the Colonization Society and other antislavery societies. In later years he was always ready to contribute money to aid fugitive slaves on their way to Canada. He likewise took great interest in the establishment of a school for colored children, then a neglected class.

For some years he was clerk of one of the business meetings of Friends, a member of the visiting committee of the Monthly Meeting School, and was also much concerned for the welfare of the religious society to which he belonged.

His convictions of honesty and fair dealing were as strong as those of his father, and his aim was to "keep a conscience void of offence."

Susanna Collins, the fifth daughter of Isaac and Rachel Collins, was born Third month 17, 1781; married Richard M. Smith, Ninth month 27, 1810; and died at the residence of her son-in-law, Matthew Howland, in New Bedford, Massachusetts, on the 6th of Sixth month, 1876, in her ninety-sixth year. She was a member and recorded minister of Friends' Meeting in Burlington, New Jersey, for more than seventy years.

She gave her heart in early life to her Saviour, whom she long loved and served, receiving a gift in the ministry, in the exercise of which she travelled quite extensively. Of an animated and cheerful disposition, she greatly enjoyed the society of her friends, and was truly given to hospitality, ever considering it one of her greatest privileges to entertain beneath her roof the servants of Christ.

Through more than fifty years of sorrowing widowhood it was her supreme desire that she and the children whom God had given her should be found walking in the truth.

In the precepts and provisions contained in the Bible, of which she was a diligent and loving student, in the biographies of departed worthies, in reading sweet hymns, in communion with the Lord's servants,—and, chief of all, in waiting upon and praying unto Him who had been her morning light, she found consolation in her declining years. And though heavy clouds were permitted at times to obscure her vision, there is good reason to believe that the Lord, out of the sometimes thick darkness, had comforted her weary yet trusting soul. "I feel something like the airs of Paradise breathing around me, an experience I never had before," was her tearful acknowledgment a short time before her death. And it is our consoling belief that the gracious language was appropriate to her, "Daughter, be of good comfort; thy faith hath made thee whole."

"Saved by the blood of Jesus" was the language impressed upon the minds of some who witnessed her gentle dismissal from the trials and conflicts of mortality to be "forever with the Lord."

MEMOIR OF ISAAC COLLINS, JR., 1787–1863.

Isaac Collins, the eleventh child of Isaac and Rachel Collins, was born in the city of Trenton, New Jersey, October 31, 1787. He was educated in Trenton, and subsequently (in 1796 the family removing to New York) at the Yearly Meeting School of Nine Partners, Dutchess County, New York, with his brother Benjamin and sisters Anna and Mary.

Having served an apprenticeship of six years with

Isaac Collins

Mott & Bowne, at the age of twenty-one years he made his first mercantile venture as supercargo to St. Mary's, Georgia, aboard the brig Dean. On his return to New York he entered into copartnership with Samuel Mott in the manufacture of flour, and went to Eastport and the Bay of Fundy on a trading voyage, having ten vessels consigned to him with cargoes which were sold successfully. He then withdrew from the business and entered into partnership, under the name of Collins & Co., with his brother Thomas.

On the 4th of Tenth month, 1810, at the age of twenty-three years, he was married to Margaret Morris, aged eighteen years, daughter of Dr. John and Abigail Morris, deceased, and went to house-keeping in New York City. The business of Collins & Co., printers and publishers of books, became very successful. They were the first in this country to employ stereotype plates. The business was largely confined to the sale of medical and educational books, avoiding the publication of novels and all books regarded as detrimental to the minds and morals of the public.

He states in his autobiography, prepared at the request of his children, that some years previously he had made a mental determination that "if his heavenly Father blessed him with the accumulation of an estate, the interest of which would maintain his family, economically, in the sphere of life in which they lived, he would retire from business and devote his life to the charities of the city." This was accomplished in his thirty-fourth year, doubtless demanding of him much courage and personal sacrifice to fulfil, in the full tide of a successful business career.

It was his belief and observation that those of his

friends who had acquired large estates had done an injustice to their sons, who, with large inheritances, lived, in most instances, in extravagance and luxury, and became selfish and useless members of society, often dissolute and intemperate.

With his brother-in-law, Stephen Grellet, he acted as executor of the estate of his father. He entered into many of the associations for the relief of the poor and destitute, aided in inaugurating the Eye Dispensary, obtaining rooms in the New York City Hospital, of which his father was one of the governors; also in the establishment of the first Saving Fund in the city of New York. In offering the first resolution in the Society for the Suppression of Pauperism, he actively aided the establishment of the House of Refuge, incorporated in 1824, where his name is venerated to this day. At this time he also devoted his time and abilities to the public school system, in both of which he was unwearyingly engaged to secure their success.

In 1828 he relinquished very reluctantly the numerous public charities in which he was engaged, receiving many letters from his friends expressive of their regrets and appreciation of his services, and removed to Philadelphia in consequence of what he feared was the precarious condition of his wife's health, it being her native city, and enjoying a milder climate.

His former public experiences had enlarged his humane conceptions of benevolence, increasing his sympathies, and he immediately resumed his philanthropic work in Philadelphia. He became a member of the Board of Managers of the House of Refuge, first opened for the reception of inmates in 1829, and to which his labors were unsparingly bestowed during the remainder of his life, so impressed was he with its great value to the community and the inmates for its far-reaching benefits.

He aided in the establishment of Haverford School in 1833, for the higher scholastic and classical education of the sons of members of the Society of Friends, subsequently incorporated as a college. He became an active participator in the management of most of the leading charities of Philadelphia, and was unceasing in his efforts to promote their prosperity and usefulness, and after this lapse of time, the large extent and prominence to which they have reached exhibits the wisdom of his selections for his sphere of philanthropic labors.

Deeply impressed with the pernicious and demoralizing effects of the lottery system of this State, in association with a few leading citizens he, for three years, labored persistently to suppress it. So deeply rooted was this legalized form of gambling among almost all classes of the people,—not less than two hundred of these offices conducting their business in Philadelphia,—that his attacks met the most determined antagonism, so that he visited Harrisburg on three occasions to obtain the legislative enactment. His life and the lives of his associates in this reform were often threatened and in danger, but their object was eventually accomplished, to the great satisfaction of these public-spirited men.

He was appointed by the Councils of the City of Philadelphia a Guardian of the Poor and Director of the Public School System. He, however, always preferred being connected with private institutions rather than those of public appointment.

The great sorrow of his life was the death of his beloved wife in 1832, after a protracted illness. She was a person of rare attractions and loveliness of character. Nine children survived her, of whom two only are living at this time.

He visited Europe on three occasions in the prosecution of his benevolent designs, one of which was to obtain funds from the exhibition and sale of Chinese curios and manufactured articles collected at large expense by his friend, Nathan Dunn, during a long residence in China, who united with him in this laudable enterprise.

On the 28th of January, 1835, he married Rebecca, daughter of John Singer, of Philadelphia, a prominent merchant and greatly-esteemed citizen. She was a minister of the religious Society of Friends, devoted to religious and charitable purposes, and continued therein until her death on the last day of April, 1892, aged eighty-seven years.

This brief outline of the philanthropic labors of Isaac Collins must close with the mention that throughout his life he was animated with the desire of promoting the religious and moral sentiments of private individuals and the public at large, and to this end was engaged in the extensive publications of the best authors on these subjects, in popular form, which were distributed throughout the country and in congressional and legislative bodies at his individual expense. He was also an active worker in the temperance and antislavery causes.

Through his personal influence and untiring efforts is to be attributed the foundation of the Institution for Feeble-minded Children, now located at Elwyn, Pennsylvania, which for many years has been successfully carried on.

He possessed a most genial and kindly nature, had a

high flow of spirits, was a student of the science of sociology, and a constant reader of books of standard and current literature, cultivating many of the refinements of life, among which he derived enjoyment in the large and beautiful flower-gardens attached to his various residences.

For many months preceding his death he was an invalid and a great sufferer, which confined him to his chamber, his death occurring in January, 1863, in the hope and confidence of a blessed immortality. The death of a man so widely known as a philanthropist induced many private and public testimonials to his worth and services, as well as from the many charitable institutions with which he was associated, all of which are affectionately preserved by his children.

Rebecca Singer, daughter of John and Anna Maria Singer, was born in Philadelphia in 1804. She joined the religious Society of Friends at the age of nineteen, and afterwards became an acceptable minister among them. She married Isaac Collins in 1835, and after his death in 1863 she removed to New York. Shortly afterwards she travelled in the ministry among Friends in England, Scotland, Ireland, France, Germany, and Norway, exhorting all everywhere to remain steadfast to their faith. During her life she visited most of the meetings of her own Society. Yet she worked in other Christian denominations, devoting much of her time to charities and reformatory institutions.

Stacy Budd Collins was the youngest but one of the children of Isaac and Rachel (Budd) Collins. He was born in Trenton, New Jersey, in 1791. In speaking of his brothers and sisters, he often said he had never seen them all together. Some of the eldest had left home before he was born. Part of his school life was spent at Friends' Seminary, at Nine Partners, New York.

He was married in 1821 to Mary Eves Dudley, daughter of Edward Dudley, of New York, formerly of Roscrea, Ireland, a lovely girl of eighteen.

A niece of my father, Rebecca Pearsall, of Philadelphia, also a very handsome girl, was bridesmaid for my mother. A furnished house in New York was taken by the young couple, and house-keeping began. This house was on a corner lot, and had a large garden. Father was always proud of a garden, and this, no doubt, was a great attraction. From this house in Prince Street they removed to 512 Broadway, where they lived many years, and where most of their children were born. This house also had a nice garden. Five daughters were born to them in succession, and then two boys. Mother died in 1837, of a slow decline, leaving four young daughters, the youngest only seven years old. One daughter,—the third, Anna,—an interesting and precocious child, died of scarlet fever in 1834, and the two little boys died in infancy.

After several years, in 1843 my father married again,—a lady from Philadelphia, Hannah W. Jenks, daughter of Joseph R. Jenks, of that city, a person well calculated to be the companion of his later years. A son and daughter came of this marriage. The son, Dr. Stacy B. Collins, and the daughter, Gertrude Collins.

In his early manhood father had travelled very extensively abroad, spending a winter in Rome and a year or more in England and on the Continent. He visited Waterloo two weeks after the battle, and was in

Paris when the allied army entered and took possession of the city. He told many interesting stories of those early days. The cultivated tastes acquired by foreign travel enriched his whole life, and gave him a wide interest in artistic matters quite unusual to men of his generation.

Father was much interested in the American Peace Society, and contributed freely to its funds. At his house in Twenty-second Street, New York, about 1853, Elihu Burritt started a local Peace Society, which continued for several years, and did good work in writing and distributing peace tracts.

I have not yet spoken of what was perhaps my father's most worthy work. I refer to his endorsement of woman's right to the ballot, and of her right to enter the learned professions. In my earliest years I can recall his saying that "every woman who paid taxes had a right to vote." It made an impression on my mind which was never effaced. He believed in the theory that "taxation without representation is tyranny."

New Jersey was his native State, and in this State from 1776 to 1807, through Quaker influence, women had been allowed to vote. Perhaps in his early youth he knew of his mother and sisters voting at elections.

To Elizabeth Blackwell, the first regularly-educated woman doctor in the United States, he was a constant and trusted friend. He sanctioned her employment as physician by his married and single daughters, and when, in 1854, she established "The New York Infirmary for Women and Children," he became one of its trustees, and retained his position for many years. The following letter was received from Dr. Blackwell when the news of his death reached her:

"DEAR MRS. HUSSEY,—My last letter from America brought me the sad intelligence of your dear father's departure from among you, and I cannot refrain from at once writing and begging you to accept the sincere sympathy which I feel for your loss.

"The disappearance of an old friend brings up the long-past times vividly to my remembrance, the time when, impelled by irresistible necessity, I strove to lead a useful but unusual life, and was able to face, with the energy of youth, both social prejudice and the hindrance of poverty.

"I love to recall those early days to show how precious your father's sympathy and support were to me in that difficult time, and how highly I respected his moral courage, in steadily, for so many years, encouraging the singular woman doctor, at whom everybody looked askance, and in passing whom so many women held their clothes aside, lest they should touch her. I know in how many good and noble things your father took part, but to me this brave advocacy of woman as physician in that early time seems the noblest of his actions.

"ELIZABETH BLACKWELL, M.D.

"LONDON, July 27, 1873."

This Infirmary, started by Dr. Blackwell, is still an important charity in New York City, and has been of great assistance to multitudes of women of all classes in the study of the practical part of their profession, and to thousands of needy women has afforded the opportunity to receive skilful treatment from physicians of their own sex.

An excellent medical college for women is now added to this Infirmary. My father was for many years a governor of the New York City Hospital, a position his father, Isaac Collins, had held before him.

He was also trustee of the New York Society Library, the oldest library in the city.

For many years he was connected with his brothers in the printing and publishing of school and other

books,* no book of pernicious influence being ever allowed to come from their press.

CORNELIA COLLINS HUSSEY.

March 30, 1893.

Joseph B. Collins, the youngest son of Isaac and Rachel Collins, was born in the city of New York, First month 30, 1794. At eighteen years of age he entered the store of his elder brothers at No. 189 Pearl Street, where he remained till he was associated with his brother Benjamin in the business of stereotyping.

"He was always engaged in business on his own account, but never allowed himself to be so absorbed by it that he could not also take his part as a citizen. He was always modest about his own exertions for the general good, and kept no memoranda of his connection with any public movement.

"One of his friends said of him that 'he was honorably distinguished among his fellows for his readiness to meet all suitable demands,' and, as a consequence, when occasion required, he was not unfrequently put on committees of relief or advice.

---

* A partial list of books printed and sold by Isaac Collins, and advertised in the "New Jersey Almanacks," viz.:

Family and School Bibles, New Testaments, Spelling-Books, Primers, Watts's Psalms, Paradise Lost, Power of Religion on the Mind, by Lindley Murray, Introduction, English Reader and Sequel to English Reader, Baxter's Saint's Everlasting Rest, Sanford and Merton, and other books for Children, Moral Philosophy, Spectator, eight volumes, The Ladies' Friend, History of America, Greek Grammar, Latin Grammar, Pike's Arithmetic, Gibson's Surveying, Emerson's Algebra, Bailey's English Dictionary, Goldsmith's England, Goldsmith's Rome, Virgil Delphini, Selectæ e profanis, Lecteur françois, Æsop's Fables, Cook's Voyages, Murray's English Grammar, Art of Speaking, Moore's Navigation, Pelew Islands, Thomson's Works, Young Man's Companion.

"His strongest interest was in the education of the young, beginning with book training, as shown in his long connection with the Public School Society, and in later years taking shape in the effort to give moral and religious instruction to the boys and girls in the Juvenile Asylum, to which he paid a daily visit for many years. He is still very cordially remembered by some inmates now living respectably, scattered about the Western country, who often recall what he said to them individually, or when he talked to the assembled school on Sunday afternoons. His simple, regular, well-occupied life won for him the regard and respect of many friends and neighbors."

E. C.

THE REUNION.

THE REUNION.

THE REUNION OF THE DESCENDANTS OF ISAAC AND RACHEL COLLINS, AT PHILADELPHIA, MAY 9, 1892.

WITH the desire of promoting a more intimate acquaintance among those descendants, and in response to a generally expressed wish from many of the family, it was proposed to hold a reunion in commemoration of the marriage of Isaac Collins with Rachel Budd, which took place on the 8th of Fifth month, 1771.

After a number of preliminary meetings were held, it was decided that the reunion should take place at the New Century Drawing-Room, No. 124 South Twelfth Street, Philadelphia, May 9, 1892.

In order to give due notice of the meeting, printed invitations were sent to every member of the family.

The following arrangement was adopted:

"The room to be opened at 5 P.M.; Frederic Collins, the chairman, to make the address of welcome; reading of the marriage certificate; a historical sketch of Isaac Collins by John Collins; an original poem; after which reminiscences and facts appropriate to the celebration by members of the family.

"It is earnestly hoped that you will accept the enclosed invitation and send an early reply to the chairman.

The following committees were appointed:

EXECUTIVE COMMITTEE.

Horace J. Smith, *Chairman*, 8 East Penn Street, Germantown.

John Collins, W. H. Collins, Edith C. Collins, Mary I. Wallen, Isaac Collins, Mary Paul Morris, Henry H. Collins, Hannah E. Collins, Helen K. Morton, Elizabeth B. Remington, Theodore H. Morris, Charles Collins, Ellen Collins.

COMMITTEE OF ARRANGEMENTS.

William Pearsall, *Chairman*, 1704 Pine Street, Philadelphia.

Clarissa S. Chase, Mary Pearsall, Mary I. Wallen, Edward M. Wistar, Elizabeth B. Remington, Frederic Chase, Letitia P. Collins, Margaret C. Wistar, Edith C. Collins, Hannah E. Collins, Mary Paul Morris, Henry H. Collins.

RECEPTION COMMITTEE.

Sarah C. Worthington, *Chairman*, 147 School Street, Germantown.

Ellen Collins, Anna B. Collins, Hannah M. Pearsall, Theodore H. Morris, Horace J. Smith, Elizabeth B. Remington, Hannah E. Collins, Elizabeth P. Smith, Joseph P. Remington, Isaac Collins.

REPORT.

At 5.30 P.M. the chairman called the meeting to order and offered the following remarks:

"My Relatives and Friends,—The pleasant position has been assigned to me this evening to preside over the exercises, which will be brief, that have been arranged by the committee in charge for this large gathering of the descendants of Isaac and Rachel Collins, for the purpose of celebrating the one hundred and twenty-first anniversary of their marriage, which occurred on the 8th of Fifth month, 1771, in the Bank Meeting-House of the Society of Friends, Philadelphia, and I most heartily welcome you here this evening on behalf of our Philadelphia relatives whose loving spirit inaugurated this happy occasion to-night.

"A century and a half has passed since our progenitor, Charles Collins, first landed in this country from his ancestral home in England, and the third, fourth, fifth, and sixth generations are numerously represented here, assembled to commemorate the worth and virtues of our ancestors, and to listen to the recital of the records which have been gathered together of their unblemished and honorable lives, and my desire is to make only a few remarks in presenting the subject.

"There is a sentiment natural to us all, of affection and of just pride in those who are our progenitors, and we feel desirous of presenting some of the leading facts of their lives. It was not that they were distinguished for heroic deeds or were prominent in the government in its formation of the then infant republic, but they are beloved by us for their Christian virtues, for their prominence in the maintenance of the principles of truth, and for their undeviating labors in the cause of philanthropy and benevolence. Their lives were without reproach, and they left their impress upon the communities in which they lived by their consistent walk of usefulness and of industry. Our admiration is excited by the successful accomplishment of their most commendable undertakings. For those blessings and traits of character in which we may claim a proper inheritance we are here to renew our interest in each other and to depend upon our friendship and fellowship. United by the same ties of blood and by a common ancestry, we extend our greetings to you this evening,—a memorable one in our lives.

"These relics * which we have here and portraits displayed, which

---

* At the reunion a number of articles were exhibited as reminiscences of Isaac and Rachel Collins or their immediate descendants. The following is a partial list:

Three family quarto Bibles printed by Isaac Collins; two volumes New Jersey Almanacs, 1771–1797; Sewel's History of the Religious Society of Quakers, Burlington, 1774; *New Jersey Gazette*, 1777–1786; commission from George III. appointing Isaac Collins printer for the Province of New Jersey; provincial paper money printed by Isaac Collins; Journal of George Fox, two volumes, 1800; scrap-book containing copies of original correspondence between Isaac Collins and others; also public documents, portraits, and silhouettes; silver medal awarded to Isaac Collins & Son (Thomas) for specimens of printing, 1804; brass knocker from front door of house on Broad Street, Burlington, New Jersey, last residence of Isaac Collins; door-latch from printing-office in Burlington, New have been treasured so carefully by those who have inherited them, portray very largely the characteristics of our ancestors. The grand old Family Bible lying on that table, which was published by our ancestor in 1791, is a monument to his memory and must so remain."

The following essay, prepared by John Collins, was then read:

"'When to the common rest that crowns our days,
  Called in the noon of life, the good man goes,
Or, full of years, and ripe in wisdom, lays
  His silver temples in their last repose;
When o'er the buds of youth the death-wind blows
  And blights the fairest; when our bitterest tears
Stream, as the eyes of those who love us close,
  We think on what they were, with many fears
  Lest goodness die with them and leave the coming years.'

"Impressed by the pathos of these lines of the poet Bryant, we desire in a few words to commemorate our virtuous ancestry upon this memorable day of our reunion. With the lapse of time the remembrance of the past must of necessity fade away, and it is eminently proper to recall some incidents in the life of him we honor, ere, in succeeding generations, they pass into oblivion. The example of such a one is surely worthy of imitation, and if virtues are transmitted to posterity, the retrospection may revive somewhat of his spirit among his numerous descendants. Be this as it may, we cannot contemplate the many excellent traits of our grandsire without a sense of gratification at the lineage whence we came and a jealous guarding of the spotless reputation of our family in coming time.

Jersey; silver knee-buckles and shoes worn by Isaac Collins; silver cups used in his family; a breadth of the wedding dress worn by Rachel Collins; a small and very plain walnut bureau which belonged to Isaac and Rachel Collins; a sampler worked by Sarah Collins, the third daughter, in 1787; portrait of Isaac Collins, by Jarvis; portrait of Margaret Morris Collins and infant daughter Margaret, by Eicholtz; portraits of various descendants and photographs of some of their residences.

"We meet to-day, a friendly band,
To greet with eye and heart and hand
Perhaps some lost relation,
And interchange a word of cheer
With numerous kinsfolk living near,
Or at some distant station.

"Descendants of a worthy sire
Whose many virtues we admire,
Whose memory we cherish;
May we revive, this gladsome day,
Old records ere they pass away
And in oblivion perish.

"'Tis said, 'the good man never dies,'
And thus our ancestor we prize,
In truly filial manner,
As one who, from his earliest youth,
Inscribed the words 'Right, Justice, Truth'
Upon his stainless banner.

"Nor must we fail to tell the worth
Of her, his dearest friend on earth,
A faithful helpmeet ever;
Whose lovely traits, with his combined,
Formed a true union of mind
Nor time nor change could sever.

"One hundred years and twenty-one
In annual circuit now have run
Since first the word was spoken
That bound the husband to his bride,
To tread life's pathway side by side,
In firmest ties unbroken.

"Aiming to profit humankind,
With means of livelihood combined,
Our grandsire's wise vocation
Was, by the aid of pen and press,
Wrong and corruption to suppress
Throughout our infant nation.

"In all his time he issued not
A single work to mar or blot
The record of life's pages,
But sought, by a consistent course,
Such truths and maxims to enforce
As might endure for ages.

"Ere yet their children, young in years,
Awaked an anxious mother's fears,
They gave them Christian training,
And long the lessons of that day
They found as watchwords on their way,
In memory retaining.

"Generous and kind, true, worthy 'Friends,'
No trace of pride or selfish ends
Marked their long lives of labor;
To rich and poor alike they showed
Their true allegiance unto God
By loving every neighbor.

"And could they now to earth return,
They surely would the good discern
In all to them related;
Some by successive ties of blood,
And others for their mutual good
Congenially mated.

"As rose the phœnix from the pyre,
Renewed in all its youthful fire,
So may this, our ovation,
Rekindle in each heart the zeal
To labor for the common weal
In this our generation.

"Then, when our life-work all is o'er
And we shall haply meet no more
As on this day's communion,
May every one partake the joy
That heaven shall give, without alloy,
In that long, grand Reunion.

"J. C."

The Chair.—That constitutes nearly all that we proposed to present before you to-day or this evening. We wish rather to show the characteristics of our ancestors than to read too many of them now. I hope at other times many more will be provided, perhaps in different form. It was determined at some of our meetings that we would not carry our records any further than for the generation immediately succeeding our grandparents, Isaac and Rachel Collins.

Our beloved relative, Rachel Grellet, wrote to John Collins a touching message concerning the reunion, which, when put into metre, was read on that occasion, viz.:

"When on our eyes the mists of death are falling,
And all our mission work on earth is done,
Oh, may we hear, that hour, the Saviour calling,
'Come, faithful one! the victory is won!'

"Laying our crowns of glory then before Him,
Or bringing in the sheaves at Harvest Home,
In swelling anthems shall our souls adore Him,
And sing His praise through endless years to come.

"Eye hath not seen what things He is preparing
In realms on high whose glory none can tell.
With many a prayer that we may all be sharing
Those lasting joys, farewell! dear friends! farewell!

"Fifth month 9, 1892."

Horace J. Smith, Chairman of the Executive Committee, after a few humorous remarks, in which he compared the "genealogical disease to an epidemic attacking people in middle life, instead of in infancy, as with teething and measles," presented a very brief memoir of Elizabeth, the fourth child of our grandparents. It will be found on page 77. H. J. Smith stated that he had been advised in a message from one of the family in California, that a new female descendant had been born there, and also sending greetings to the reunion.

The Chair.—It has been suggested that it would be very desirable to have these different records of our family preserved and put in a suitable form to be printed and distributed among our families, not only for our own use, but for the more familiar knowledge of them for ourselves and all those who may come after us. There are not less than two hundred here, and this thing may not occur again for another century. I would submit it to you whether it would not be desirable and advisable to have this suggestion carried out, and that the material be arranged and placed in the hands of a committee of a few of our relatives, so that such a book may be prepared.

The following preamble and resolution were then passed unanimously:

"Whereas, A number of interesting and valuable historical sketches have been presented to this meeting, portraying the characteristics of Isaac and Rachel Collins, which should be preserved for the benefit of descendants, it is hereby

"*Resolved,* That these records and reminiscences, and others that may be obtained, be arranged for publication, for the use of the family, and that a committee of three be appointed by the chairman of this meeting, and that they be hereby authorized to take charge of the whole subject, and to print in a book such papers as, in their judgment, may be advisable."

The Chair.—Our cousin, Horace J. Smith, always alive to the enjoyment of every person, has advised me to call attention to the following notice, viz.:

"Special Excursion to Burlington of the members of the Collins Reunion, May 10, 1892, on the steamboat Riverside, chartered for the occasion.

"PROGRAM.

"10 A.M.—Leave Walnut Street wharf, Delaware River.

"11 A.M.—Lunch.

"12 M.—Arrive at Burlington. Objects of interest within walking distance: Burlington Library, Friends' Meeting-House and burial-grounds, residences of Margaret M. Smith, Stephen Grellet, Isaac Collins, Margaret Morris.

"3 P.M.—Leave Burlington.

"5 P.M.—Arrive at Walnut Street wharf."

After a vote of thanks had been moved to the Committee of Arrangements for the reunion and entertainment, and a remark made by John Collins, at the suggestion of the chair, that, having lived many years longer in Burlington than any one present, he would gladly go on the excursion and escort the company to any place desired,

On motion, the meeting adjourned.

The 10th of May, 1892, dawned beautifully, as did the preceding one, when a party of relatives and others assembled on the little steamer Riverside, *en route* to the old city of Burlington, made memorable to us as the residence of our worthy grandparents for a number of years. To some the scenery was entirely new, while to others, to whom it had been long familiar, the interest of the occasion made the various localities seem more home-like than ever.

The party, disembarking, passed up the main street in different groups, as fancy led them. One remarked that the present population of the town seemed to show but little interest in the visit of the descendants of a former citizen, once so prominent in its earlier history and so warmly welcomed when he returned to pass among his friends the residue of his life. The first stop was to look at the site of the Collins printing-house; then, after a view of his first residence, at the corner of Main and Union (or, as it was once called, Market) Streets, the company divided, some anxious to see the library, while others pressed on up Main Street, passing the wall-enclosed Friends' Meeting-House and the former residence of Margaret Morris Smith. Again there was a separation; but the majority turning up Broad Street, wended their way slowly to the old residence at the corner of York and Broad Streets, which had been prepared for the visit through the courtesy of Dr. Gauntt, the present owner. Here the party wandered about, looking into every nook and corner with prying curiosity, while some, who knew every part of the establishment, explained the use of every room, or noticed the changes that had been made since the illustrious occupant had lived therein. Some lingered a long time, as if to catch the inspiration of the place; others were sooner satisfied, and left to visit other spots. Photographers, as usual, were there, and several pictures were taken, including those of persons who had in days of "auld lang syne," as children, frequented the plainly-furnished rooms or enjoyed the large and fruitful garden. Most of those present felt that it was probably the last time they would see the interior of the dwelling of one of whose reputation they were so proud. A photograph of relatives at the door was taken, and others of the house, showing the changes that have taken place during the past seventy-five years.

A few of the visitors, taking carriages, rode out to

see West Hill, Oxmead, and other residences once familiar to our grandfather, where he spent many a sociable and happy hour. Some of the party went to the graveyard to spend a few minutes around the last resting-place of our ancestors. In one line lie his remains, those of his second wife, and seven of the family of his second son, Thomas. It would have been well if all the descendants could have assembled around that grass-grown mound to muse upon the useful deeds and peaceful death of him in commemoration of whom they had visited one of the scenes of his labors.

Other places of interest were viewed by the excursionists, and at the appointed hour they returned in the Riverside. Reminiscences of various members of the Collins family or of noted personages were brought out during the return trip, adding interest to the excursion, and the unanimous feeling, on reaching the wharf at Philadelphia, was that the day had been pleasurably and profitably spent, leaving an ineffaceable impression on every one, of the old Burlington home of our worthy progenitor.

GENEALOGY.

GENEALOGY.

ISAAC COLLINS, son of Charles and Sarah Collins, was born in New Castle County, Delaware, Second month 16th, 1746, and died in Burlington, New Jersey, Third month 21st, 1817.

RACHEL BUDD, daughter of Thomas and Rebecca Budd, was born at Mount Holly, New Jersey, Eleventh month 17th, 1750, and died at Westchester, New York, Ninth month 15th, 1805.

ISAAC COLLINS and RACHEL BUDD were married at the Bank Meeting-House, on Front Street above Arch Street, Philadelphia, Fifth month 8th, 1771.

ISAAC COLLINS and DEBORAH SMITH (widow of Benjamin Smith and daughter of Margaret Morris, born in 1759) were married in Burlington, New Jersey, Eleventh month 9th, 1808. She died Third month 17th, 1822.

CHILDREN OF ISAAC AND RACHEL COLLINS.

1, Rebecca; 2, Charles; 3, Sarah; 4, Elizabeth; 5, Rachel; 6, Thomas; 7, Susanna; 8, William; 9, Benjamin Say; 10, Anna Say; 11, Isaac; 12, Mary; 13, Stacy Budd; 14, Joseph Budd.*

II.—1. REBECCA COLLINS, born 6 mo. 1st, 1772; married Stephen Grellet, 1 mo. 11th, 1804; died 3 mo. 9th, 1861, aged 88 years, 9 months.

Issue:

III.—1. Rachel Grellet, born 12 mo. 21st, 1810.

* The total sum of the ages of the fourteen children is one thousand and twenty-three years, eleven months, and sixteen days; the average age being seventy-three years, one month, and twenty days.

II.—2. CHARLES COLLINS, born 1 mo. 14th, 1774; married Margaret Bullock, 4th mo., 1801; died 12 mo. 27th, 1843.

Issue:

III.—1. Edith Collins, born 8 mo. 13th, 1803; died 8 mo. 25th, 1873.

III.—2. Rachel Collins, born 1 mo. 22nd, 1805; died 7 mo. 21st, 1878.

III.—3. George B. Collins, born 2 mo. 14th, 1807; died 1 mo. 6th, 1854.

III.—4. Edward Collins, born 5 mo. 8th, 1810; died 2 mo. 1st, 1817.

II.—3. SARAH COLLINS, born 6 mo. 2nd, 1775; married Nathaniel Hawxhurst, 7 mo. 13th, 1836; died 4 mo. 23rd, 1855.

II.—4. ELIZABETH COLLINS, born 12 mo. 13th, 1776; married Robert Pearsall, 1797; died 11 mo. 11th, 1857.

Issue:

III.—1. Robert Pearsall, Jr., born 11 mo. 9th, 1798; died 1 mo. 23rd, 1866.

III.—2. Rachel C. Pearsall, born 12 mo. 29th, 1800; died 8 mo. 2nd, 1873.

III.—3. Mary Pearsall, born 10 mo. 20th, 1802; died 8 mo. 24th, 1886.

III.—4. Rebecca Grellet Pearsall, born 6 mo. 18th, 1805; died 1 mo. 20th, 1864.

III.—5. Elizabeth Pearsall, born 9 mo. 16th, 1812; died 6 mo. 12th, 1829.

III.—1. ROBERT PEARSALL, JR., 2nd, married Ann Shoemaker, 1 mo. 5th, 1825.

Issue:

IV.—1. Elizabeth Pearsall, born 10 mo. 6th, 1825; died 6 mo. 13th, 1827.

IV.—2. Robert Pearsall, born 11 mo. 25th, 1827; died 1 mo. 5th, 1849.

IV.—3. Henry Pearsall, born 5 mo. 6th, 1830; died 7 mo. 9th, 1831.

IV.—4. Francis Pearsall, born 5 mo. 1st, 1832; died 10 mo. 5th, 1883.

IV.—5. Sarah Pearsall, born 2 mo. 20th, 1834; died 2 mo. 3rd, 1835.

IV.—6. William Pearsall, born 2 mo. 24th, 1836; married Hannah M. Parrish, 11 mo. 2nd, 1861.

Issue:

V.—1. Robert Pearsall, Jr., born 2 mo. 4th, 1863.

V.—2. William Parrish Pearsall, born 3 mo. 7th, 1866; married Violette B. Morel, San Francisco, 5 mo. 14th, 1890.

Issue:

VI.—1. Robert Pearsall, Jr., born 10 mo. 10th, 1891.

V.—3. Elizabeth Parrish Pearsall, born 5 mo. 6th, 1869; married William West Frazier, Jr., 12 mo. 3rd, 1889.

Issue:

VI.—1. William West Frazier (3rd), born 4 mo. 12th, 1891.

V.—4. Mary Pearsall, born 1 mo. 14th, 1873.

III.—1. ROBERT PEARSALL, JR., 2nd, married Emily Fell (his second wife), 12 mo. 28th, 1842.

Issue:

IV.—1. Emily Elizabeth Pearsall, born 2 mo. 13th, 1844; married Charles Poultney Dawson, 10 mo. 28th, 1863.

Issue:

V.—1. Helen Dawson, born 8 mo. 3rd, 1864.

V.—2. Emily Fell Dawson, born 6 mo. 25th, 1866.

III.—1. ROBERT PEARSALL, JR., 2nd, married Eleanor H. Warder (his third wife), 5 mo. 23rd, 1849.

Issue:

IV.—1. Ann Warder Pearsall, born 6 mo. 2nd, 1851.
IV.—2. Mary Pearsall, born 2 mo. 4th, 1853.
IV.—3. Henrietta Warder Pearsall, born 10 mo. 7th, 1854.
IV.—4. Ellen Warder Pearsall, born 11 mo. 17th, 1860; married Charles Albert Longstreth, 11 mo. 4th, 1885.

III.—2. RACHEL C. PEARSALL married John Jay Smith, 4 mo. 12th, 1821.

Issue:

IV.—1. Lloyd P. Smith, born 2 mo. 6th, 1822; married Hannah E. Jones, 10 mo. 13th, 1846; died 7 mo. 2nd, 1886.
IV.—2. Albanus Logan Smith, born 9 mo. 30th, 1823; died 3 mo. 29th, 1842.
IV.—3. Elizabeth Pearsall Smith, born 7 mo. 29th, 1825.
IV.—4. Robert P. Smith, born 2 mo. 1st, 1827; married Hannah Whitall, daughter of John M. and Mary Whitall, 6 mo. 25th, 1851.

Issue:

V.—1. Gulielma Maria Smith, born 7 mo. 29, 1852; died 12 mo. 25, 1857.
V.—2. Frank Whitall Smith, born 8 mo. 12th, 1854; died 8 mo. 8th, 1872.
V.—3. Mary Whitall Smith, born 2 mo. 14th, 1864; married Benjamin Francis Conn Costelloe, of England, 9 mo. 13th, 1885.

Issue:

VI.—1. Rachel Pearsall Conn Costelloe, born 6 mo. 4th, 1887.
VI.—2. Katharine Elizabeth Conn Costelloe, born 3 mo. 11th, 1889.

V.—4. Lloyd Logan Smith, born 10 mo. 18th, 1865.
V.—5. Alys Whitall Smith, born 7 mo. 21st, 1867.
V.—6. Rachel Pearsall Smith, Jr., born 10 mo. 6th, 1868; died 2 mo. 7th, 1880.

IV.—5. Gulielma Maria, born 7 mo. 30th, 1829; died 12 mo. 25th, 1835.

IV.—6. Horace J. Smith, born 12 mo. 9th, 1832; married Margaret Longstreth, 12 mo. 9th, 1857.

Issue:

V.—1. Albanus Longstreth Smith, born 3 mo. 29th, 1859; married Emma Brooks Mellor, 10 mo. 20th, 1885.

Issue:

VI.—1. Mayburry Mellor Smith, born 7 mo. 30th, 1888.

VI.—2. Lloyd Mellor Smith, born 9 mo. 25th, 1890.

V.—2. Mary B. Longstreth Smith, born 8 mo. 30th, 1863; died in Paris, France, 2 mo. 19th, 1884.

V.—3. Wilson Longstreth Smith, born 4 mo. 28th, 1867.

V.—4. Margaret Longstreth Smith, born 10 mo. 20th, 1871.

IV.—7. Margaret Hill Smith, daughter of John J. and Rachel P. Smith, born 10 mo. 14th, 1840; died 12 mo. 27th, 1840.

III.—3. Rebecca Grellet Pearsall, daughter of Robert and Elizabeth Pearsall (II.), born 6 mo. 18th, 1805; married Dr. Samuel George Morton, 10 mo. 20th, 1827; died 1 mo. 20th, 1864.

Issue:

IV.—1. James St. Clair Morton (Brigadier-General), born 9 mo. 24th, 1829; killed in battle at Petersburg, Va., June 17, 1864.

IV.—2. Robert Pearsall Morton, born 5 mo. 22nd, 1831; married Julia V. Wiltbank, 10 mo. 1st, 1868.

Issue:

V.—1. Julia Carleton Morton, born 1 mo. 30th, 1870; died 3 mo. 25th, 1872.

V.—2. Robert Pearsall Morton, born 8 mo. 1st, 1871.

IV.—3. George Morton, born 12 mo. 21st, 1832; died 5 mo. 14th, 1850.

IV.—4. Thomas George Morton, born 8 mo. 8th, 1835; married Ann Jenks Kirkbride, 11 mo. 12th, 1861.

Issue:

V.—1. Helen Kirkbride Morton, born 11 mo. 5th, 1862.

V.—2. Thomas Story Kirkbride Morton, born 1 mo. 18th, 1865; married Mary Waln Wistar Brown, 2 mo. 9th, 1888.

Issue:

VI.—1. Samuel George Morton, born 12 mo. 2nd, 1888; died 1 mo. 31st, 1889.

VI.—2. Mary Waln Wistar Morton, born 11 mo. 26th, 1889.

VI.—3. Thomas George Morton, born 10 mo. 17th, 1891.

V.—3. Samuel George Morton, born 3 mo. 20th, 1867; died 5 mo. 2nd, 1874.

V.—4. Bertha St. Clair Morton, born 10 mo. 16th, 1870; married John Constable Gittings, 1 mo. 6th, 1892.

V.—5. James St. Clair Morton, born 5 mo. 6th, 1872; died 9 mo. 18th, 1880.

V.—6. Arthur Villiers Morton, born 9 mo. 2nd, 1873.

V.—7. Isabella Fitz-Gerald Morton, born 3 mo. 5th, 1879.

IV.—5. Anna Morton, born 11 mo. 4th, 1838; married Thomas Harrison Montgomery, 10 mo. 31st, 1860.

Issue:

V.—1. Rebecca Morton Montgomery, born 6 mo. 29th, 1862.

V.—2. Mary White Montgomery, born 8 mo. 7th, 1864.

V.—3. James Alan Montgomery, born 6 mo. 13th, 1866.

V.—4. Samuel George Morton Montgomery, born 5 mo. 11th, 1868.

V.—5. Anna Morton Montgomery, born 2 mo. 7th, 1870.

V.—6. Thomas Harrison Montgomery, born 3 mo. 5th, 1873.

V.—7. William White Montgomery, born 10 mo. 28th, 1874.

V.—8. Charles Mortimer Montgomery, born 10 mo. 23rd, 1876.

V.—9. Emily Hollingsworth Montgomery, born 10 mo. 23rd, 1882.

IV.—6. William Henry Harrison Morton, born 4 mo. 2nd, 1841; died 4 mo. 26th, 1841.

IV.—7. Mary Elizabeth Morton, born 10 mo. 16th, 1842; died 9 mo. 1st, 1882.

IV.—8. Algernon Morton, born 4 mo. 18th, 1845; married Mary Grier Cope, 12 mo. 14th, 1876; died 3 mo. 25th, 1878.

Issue :

V.—1. John Edmund Cope Morton, born 9 mo. 19th, 1877.

IV.—9. Charles Mortimer Morton, born 2 mo. 11th, 1848; married Sarah Glen Douglas Emory, 10 mo. 10th, 1883, who died 3 mo. 21st, 1885.

Issue :

V.—1. Charles Mortimer Morton, Jr., born 3 mo. 21st, 1885; died 3 mo. 21st, 1885.

II.—5. RACHEL COLLINS, born 9 mo. 8th, 1777; died 9 mo. 12th, 1778.

II.—6. THOMAS COLLINS, born 3 mo. 3rd, 1779; married Ann Abbott, 9 mo. 2nd, 1812; died 1 mo. 22nd, 1859.

Issue :

III.—1. John Collins, born 3 mo. 15th, 1814; married Anna Baily, only daughter of Joshua and Elizabeth L. Baily, 10 mo. 2nd, 1839.

Issue :

IV.—1. Elizabeth Baily Collins, born 11 mo. 10th, 1840; married Joseph P. Remington, 6 mo. 3rd, 1874.

Issue :

V.—1. Arthur Hart Remington, born 9 mo. 18th, 1875.

V.—2. Joseph Percy Remington, born 2 mo. 15th, 1877.

V.—3. William Procter Remington, born 3 mo. 13th, 1879.

V.—4. Anna Collins Remington, born 4 mo. 11th, 1881.

V.—5. Elizabeth Baily Remington, born 4 mo. 14th, 1888.

IV.—2. Mary L. Collins, born 8 mo. 4th, 1848; married James F. Wood, 11 mo. 9th, 1875.

Issue :

V.—1. William M. Wood, born 8 mo. 13th, 1876.

V.—2. Harold B. Wood, born 3 mo. 23rd, 1878.

IV.—3. William Albert Collins, only son, born 7 mo. 11th, 1852; died 6 mo. 10th, 1859.

IV.—4. Caroline Baily Collins, born 4 mo. 29th, 1858; married Eugene M. Aaron, 8 mo. 28th, 1875.

8

Issue:

V.—1. Joseph Murray Aaron, born 10 mo. 29th, 1876.

V.—2. Frederic Eugene Aaron, born 12 mo. 30th, 1877.

V.—3. Charles Francis Aaron, born 1 mo. 25th, 1879; died 8 mo. 3rd, 1879.

IV.—5 and 6. Sarah Loyd and Fannie Baily Collins were born 4 mo. 17th, 1863; the latter died 7 mo. 22nd, 1865.

III.—2. Arthur Collins, born 10 mo. 3rd, 1815; married Sarah Ivins, 5 mo. 5th, 1847; died 8 mo. 28th, 1871.

Issue:

IV.—1. Arthur T. Collins, born 7 mo. 21st, 1848; married Elizabeth Woolston, 9 mo. 5th, 1878.

Issue:

V.—1. Marian Collins, born 10 mo. 28th, 1880; died 12 mo. 8th, 1888.

V.—2. Benjamin Woolston Collins, born 3 mo. 17th, 1889.

V.—3. Arthur Collins, born 9 mo. 29th, 1891.

IV.—2. Mary Ivins Collins, born 6 mo. 7th, 1852; married Jarvis Royal Wallen 8 mo. 27th, 1879.

Issue:

V.—1. Seeley Arthur Wallen, born 6 mo. 16th, 1880.

V.—2. Eva Wallen, born 5 mo. 8th, 1882.

IV.—3. Walter A. Collins, born 8 mo. 26th, 1857.

III.—3. Charles Collins, born 10 mo. 29th, 1817; died 9 mo. 14th, 1824.

III.—4. Thomas Abbott Collins, born 6 mo. 11th, 1819; died 11 mo. 27th, 1840.

III.—5. Francis Collins, born 4 mo. 6th, 1821; married Anna Whitehead, 1 mo. 29th, 1850; died 6 mo. 2nd, 1880.

Issue:

IV.—1. Thomas Collins, born 1 mo. 9th, 1853.

IV.—2. Helen Collins, born 4 mo. 20th, 1855.

IV.—3. Frances Collins, born 4 mo. 22nd, 1857; married Anthony Morris Hall, 3 mo. 29th, 1887.

Issue:

V.—1. Ethel Hall, born 3 mo. 12th, 1888.

V.—2. Margaretta Hall, born 3 mo. 26th, 1890.

IV.—4. Charles W. Collins, born 2 mo. 27th, 1860.

IV.—5. Abbott Collins, born 6 mo. 13th, 1862.

IV.—6. Edward Collins, born 12 mo. 28th, 1866; died 12 mo. 21st, 1875.

III.—6. Albert Collins, born 6 mo. 18th, 1825; married Elizabeth A. Leaver, 4 mo. 13th, 1853; died 11 mo. 8th, 1854.

Issue:

IV.—1. Henry Albert Collins, born 2 mo. 9th, 1854; married Florence M. Hurd, 6 mo. 5th, 1878.

Issue:

V.—1. Milton Collins, born 11 mo. 18th, 1881; died 9 mo. 3rd, 1883.

V.—2. Clyde H. Collins, born 8 mo. 17th, 1883.

II.—7. SUSANNA COLLINS, born 3 mo. 17th, 1781; married Richard Morris Smith, 9 mo. 27th, 1810. She died 6 mo. 6th, 1876, in the ninety-sixth year of her age.

Issue:

III.—1. Maria Smith, born 9 mo. 16th, 1812; married Josiah Richardson Reeve, 9 mo. 22, 1831.

Issue:

IV.—1. Susan S. Reeve, born 1 mo. 25th, 1833; died 10 mo. 4th, 1866.

IV.—2. Richardson S. Reeve, born 4 mo. 9th, 1840; married Josephine Augusta Clay, 1 mo. 30th, 1878.

Issue:

V.—1. Herbert Ely Reeve, born 12 mo. 8th, 1878.

V.—2. Maria Smith Reeve, born 1 mo. 18th, 1880.

V.—3. Richardson Henry Reeve, born 11 mo. 3rd, 1883.

IV.—3. Josiah Reeve, born 11 mo. 27th, 1842; married Jennetta Elizabeth Johnson, 11 mo. 2nd, 1870.

Issue:

V.—1. Percival Johnson Reeve, born 9 mo. 25th, 1871.

V.—2. Susan Smith Reeve, born 12 mo. 16th, 1873.

V.—3. Josiah Stanley Reeve, born 3 mo. 18th, 1878.

IV.—4. George Dillwyn Reeve, born 9 mo. 27th, 1845; married Sarah Cadwallader Comfort, 9 mo. 27th, 1877.

Issue:

V.—1. Rachel Comfort Reeve, born 5 mo. 13th, 1880.

V.—2. Margaret Morris Reeve, born 11 mo. 8th, 1881.

IV.—5. Maria Elizabeth Reeve, born 3 mo. 22nd, 1849; died 12 mo. 12th, 1889.

III.—2. Rachel Collins Smith, born 5 mo. 6th, 1816; married Matthew Howland, of New Bedford, Mass., 9 mo. 8th, 1842.

Issue:

IV.—1. Susan Dillwyn Howland, born 1 mo. 25th, 1845; died 10 mo. 4th, 1851.

IV.—2. Richard S. Howland, born 7 mo. 11th, 1847; married Mary Hoppin, 12 mo. 23rd, 1869.

Issue:

V.—1. Frederic Howland, born 1 mo. 10th, 1871.

V.—2. Rachel S. Howland, born 12 mo. 17th, 1873.

V.—3. Richard Stanley Howland, born 8 mo. 13th, 1875.

V.—4. Courtlandt H. Howland, born 6 mo. 5th, 1877.

V.—5. Reginald H. Howland, born 3 mo. 23rd, 1880.

IV.—3. Matthew M. Howland, born 12 mo. 14th, 1850.

IV.—4. William Dillwyn Howland, born 3 mo. 14th, 1853; married Caroline Child, 9 mo. 22nd, 1875.

Issue:

V.—1. Llewellyn Howland, born 10 mo. 9th, 1877.

III.—3. Dillwyn Smith, born 4 mo. 2nd, 1818; married Elizabeth M. Morris, 7 mo. 6th, 1848; died 9 mo. 10th, 1891.

II.—8. William Collins, born 8 mo. 18th, 1782; married Ann Newbold Bispham, widow of Stacy Budd Bispham, 10 mo. 29th, 1818. He died 8 mo. 22nd, 1843.

Issue :

III.—1. Susanna Collins, born 8 mo. 25th, 1819; married George W. Hunter, 6 mo. 15th 1842.

Issue :

IV.—1. Helen Hunter, born 3 mo. 26th, 1843.

IV.—2. Anna Hunter, born 8 mo. 11th, 1844.

IV.—3. Mary Hunter, born 10 mo. 4th, 1845; died 3 mo. 3rd, 1847.

IV.—4. William Collins Hunter, born 11 mo. 4th, 1846; died 5 mo. 22nd, 1848.

IV.—5. Emily Hunter, born 6 mo. 27th, 1848; died 6 mo. 27th, 1874.

IV.—6. Susan Hunter, born 11 mo. 10th, 1849.

IV.—7. George Kenelm Hunter, born 12 mo. 3rd, 1851; married Sophie Keen, 1 mo. 14th, 1878.

Issue :

V.—1. William Matlack Hunter, born 6 mo. 24th, 1879.

V.—2. George Washington Hunter, born 1 mo. 23rd, 1882; died 2 mo. 25th, 1888.

V.—3. Mary Hunter, born 11 mo. 6th, 1883.

V.—4. Walter Lynde Hunter, born 12 mo. 15th, 1884.

V.—5. Anna Newbold Hunter, born 6 mo. 26th, 1886.

V.—6. Marjorie Grellet Hunter, born 12 mo. 11th, 1887.

V.—7. Beatrice Kenelm Hunter, born 5 mo. 7th, 1889.

V.—8. Jessie Dorothy Hunter, born 12 mo. 2nd, 1890.

IV.—8. Martha Hunter, born 6 mo. 22nd, 1853; married Francis J. Welsh, 1875; died 7 mo. 18th, 1878.

Issue :

V.—1. Henry Hunter Welsh, born 11 mo. 23rd, 1876.

V.—2. John Rice Welsh,
V.—3. William Walter Welsh, } born 7 mo. 5th, 1878; died 8 mo. 20th, 1878, and 8 mo. 3rd, 1878.

IV.—9. Charles Joseph Hunter, born 6 mo. 25th, 1856; died 7 mo. 7th, 1856.

IV.—10. Harriet Lynde Hunter, born 3 mo. 12th, 1859; died 4 mo. 3rd, 1867.

IV.—11. Henry Reed Hunter, born 6 mo. 22nd, 1860; died 7 mo. 7th, 1861.

III.—2. Euphemia Collins, born 4 mo. 19th, 1821; died 9 mo. 27th, 1822.

III.—3. Mary Anna Collins, born 3 mo. 7th, 1823.

III.—4. Emily Collins, born 8 mo. 17th, 1825.

III.—5. Charles B. Collins, born 11 mo. 3rd, 1826; died 9 mo. 23d, 1832.

III.—6. Augustus Collins, born 10 mo. 27th, 1829; died 7 mo. 15th, 1830.

II.—9. Benjamin Say Collins, born 3 mo. 7th, 1784; married Hannah Bowne, 8 mo. 15th, 1810; died 8 mo. 26th, 1857.

Issue:

III.—1. Elizabeth Bowne Collins, born 9 mo. 6th, 1811.

III.—2. Robert Bowne Collins, born 4 mo. 17th, 1813; married Margaretta C. Murray, 5 mo. 13th, 1846.

Issue:

IV.—1. Lindley M. Collins, born 2 mo. 23rd, 1847; died 10 mo. 11th, 1875.

IV.—2. Elizabeth B. Collins, born 9 mo. 11th, 1848; died 5 mo. 4th, 1879.

IV.—3. Jane Murray Collins, born 7 mo. 28th, 1850; died 6 mo. 8th, 1852.

IV.—4. Margaretta M. Collins, born 6 mo. 12th, 1861.

III.—3. William Bowne Collins, born 9 mo. 3rd, 1815; married Ann Griffin, 6 mo. 8th, 1842; died 6 mo. 24th, 1890.

Issue:

IV.—1. Emily Collins, born 9 mo. 12th, 1844; died 1 mo. 24th, 1864.

IV.—2. Lucy Collins, born 7 mo. 14th, 1848; died 1 mo. 10th, 1864.

IV.—3. Cornelia Collins, born 5 mo. 22nd, 1850; married Benjamin Tatham, 2 mo. 3rd, 1891.

III.—William Bowne Collins married Mary Griffin, his second wife, 7 mo. 17th, 1856.

Issue:

IV.—1. William Henry Collins, born 10 mo. 23rd, 1859.

III.—4. Mary Collins, born 7 mo. 16th, 1817; died 6 mo. 20th, 1826.

III.—5. Rebecca Collins, born 5 mo. 19th, 1819; married Benjamin Tatham, 6 mo. 10th, 1847.

Issue:

IV.—1. Hannah Tatham, born 5 mo. 7th, 1848; died 7 mo. 9th, 1867.

IV.—2. William Tatham, born 7 mo. 10th, 1850.

IV.—3. Fanny Tatham, born 12 mo. 12th, 1852; died 2 mo. 29th, 1853.

IV.—4. Charles Tatham, born 9 mo. 3rd, 1854.

IV.—5. Francis Tatham, born 3 mo. 19th, 1858.

IV.—6. Edwin Tatham, born 11 mo. 18th, 1859.

III.—6. Edward Collins, born 2 mo. 2nd, 1821; died 6 mo. 18th, 1837.

III.—7. Benjamin Collins, born 12 mo. 1st, 1822.

III.—8. Richard Smith Collins, born 1 mo. 13th, 1825; married Sarah Willets, 4 mo. 9th, 1856.

Issue:

IV.—1. Maria Willets Collins, born 11 mo. 10th, 1858; married Dr. Joshua L. Barton, 8 mo. 11th, 1882.

IV.—2. Hannah Collins, born 7 mo. 18th, 1860.

IV.—3. Stephen Willets Collins, born 12 mo. 25th, 1862.

IV.—4. Benjamin Collins, born 11 mo. 14th, 1864; married Esther Carpenter, 11 mo. 12th, 1890.

Issue:

V.—1. Emma Elizabeth Collins, born 1 mo. 16th, 1892.

IV.—5. Sarah Collins, born 7 mo. 7th, 1866.

IV.—6. Richard Collins, born 11 mo. 16th, 1868.

IV.—7. Minturn Post Collins, born 9 mo. 7th, 1870.

IV.—8. Charles Collins, born 9 mo. 8th, 1872.

III.—9. Mary Collins, born 5 mo. 17th, 1828.

III.—10. Charles Collins, born 6 mo. 5th, 1830.

II.—10. ANNA SAY COLLINS, daughter of Isaac and Rachel Collins, born 3 mo. 6th, 1786; died 5 mo. 19th, 1872.

II.—11. ISAAC COLLINS, son of Isaac and Rachel Collins, born 10 mo. 31st, 1787; married Margaret Morris, 10 mo. 4th, 1810, who died 4 mo. 22nd, 1832. He afterwards married Rebecca Singer, 1 mo. 28th, 1835, who died 4 mo. 30th, 1892. Isaac Collins died 1 mo. 15th, 1863.

Issue of Isaac and Margaret M. Collins.

III.—1. William Morris Collins, born 7 mo. 21st, 1811; married Eliza C. Cope, 11 mo. 7th, 1839; died 10 mo. 30th, 1864.

Issue:

IV.—1. Mary Ann Collins, born 9 mo. 16th, 1841.

IV.—2. Lydia Cope Collins, born 4 mo. 1st, 1845; married John B. Wood, 5 mo. 8th, 1867.

Issue:

V.—1. Ellen C. Wood, born 6 mo. 19th, 1868.

V.—2. Horatio Curtis Wood, born 2 mo. 5th, 1870.

V.—3. Arthur Morris Wood, born 11 mo. 17th, 1873.

V.—4. Edward Cope Wood, born 1 mo. 12th, 1880.

V.—5. John Beaumont Wood, born 6 mo. 2nd, 1886; died 10 mo. 2nd, 1887.

IV.—3. Margaret Cooper Collins, born 3 mo. 9th, 1852; married Edward M. Wistar, 11 mo. 16th, 1876.

Issue:

V.—1. Thomas Wistar, born 10 mo. 18th, 1877.

V.—2. Caspar Wistar, born 11 mo. 18th, 1880.

V.—3. Elizabeth Cope Wistar, born 11 mo. 11th, 1884.

III.—2. Martha Lawrie Collins, born 7 mo. 19th, 1813; married John B. Bispham, 10 mo. 3rd, 1833; died 5 mo. 6th, 1887.

Issue:

IV.—1. John Bispham, born 6 mo. 25th, 1834; died 3 mo. 9th, 1842.

IV.—2. Margaret Bispham, born 4 mo. 21st, 1836; married

Hugh Munroe Dewees, 6 mo. 7th, 1881; he died 2 mo. 8th, 1887.

IV.—3. William Bispham, born 5 mo. 5th, 1838; married Laura Wistar, 10 mo. 7th, 1863.

Issue:

V.—1. Clarence Wyatt Bispham, born 7 mo. 16th, 1865.

IV.—4. Henry Collins Bispham, born 6 mo. 9th, 1841; married Ida Tilghman Lowry, 6 mo. 1st, 1871; died at Rome, 12 mo. 22nd, 1883.

Issue:

V.—1. Avice de Heyton Bispham, born 5 mo. 31st, 1872; died 6 mo. 13th, 1884.

V.—2. Henry Carroll Bispham, born 1 mo. 26th, 1875; died 4 mo. 1st, 1879.

III.—3. Gulielma Maria Collins, born 8 mo. 28th, 1815; married Philip B. Chase, 6 mo. 5th, 1839; died 2 mo. 4th, 1867.

Issue:

IV.—1. Henry Collins Chase, born 7 mo. 18th, 1840; died 7 mo. 21st, 1840.

IV.—2. Frederic Chase, born 9 mo. 1st, 1841; married Clarissa S. Hart, 11 mo. 30th, 1865.

Issue:

V.—1. Frederic Albert Chase, born 11 mo. 20th, 1866; died 6 mo. 24th, 1868.

V.—2. Julia Maria Chase, born 7 mo. 29th, 1868.

V.—3. Clarissa Townley Chase, born 1 mo. 6th, 1873.

V.—4. Samuel Hart Chase, born 3 mo. 16th, 1874.

V.—5. Mabel Bertha Chase, born 9 mo. 19th, 1875.

IV.—3. Philip Francis Chase, born 11 mo. 29th, 1843; married Elizabeth La Conte Penington, 10 mo. 26th, 1871; died 8 mo. 6th, 1880.

IV.—4. William M. Chase, born 5 mo. 15th, 1847; married Josephine Almaida McMackin, 10 mo. 2nd, 1873.

Issue:

V.—1. Maria Collins Chase, born 12 mo. 15th, 1877; died 5 mo. 13th, 1888.

IV.—5. Morton Chase, born 11 mo. 11th, 1850; married Annie Rhoads, 11 mo. 5th, 1874. She died 4 mo. 26th, 1888.

Issue:

V.—1. Maris Rhoads Chase, born 11 mo. 4th, 1875; died 2 mo. 20th, 1882.

V.—2. Susan C. Chase, born 2 mo. 24th, 1877; died 2 mo. 24th, 1882.

V.—3. Morton Hazen Collins Chase, born 2 mo. 18th, 1884.

V.—4. Ann Eliza Chase, born 9 mo. 22nd, 1886.

IV.—6. Ernest Hazen Chase, born 1 mo. 1st, 1854.

III.—4. Henry Hill Collins, born 2 mo. 3rd, 1818; died 7 mo. 20th, 1840.

III.—5. Alfred M. Collins, born 1 mo. 11th, 1820; married Hannah R. Evans, 11 mo. 22nd, 1843.

Issue:

IV.—1. Henry Hill Collins, born 9 mo. 4th, 1844; married Edith E. Conrad, 2 mo. 23rd, 1869.

Issue:

V.—1. Henry H. Collins, born 5 mo. 29th, 1873.

V.—2. Alfred M. Collins, born 5 mo. 3rd, 1876.

V.—3. Edith Conrad Collins, born 12 mo. 11th, 1886.

IV.—2. Elizabeth Richards Collins, born 10 mo. 24th, 1846; died 12 mo. 3rd, 1846.

IV.—3. Fanny T. Collins, born 10 mo. 30th, 1850; died 2 mo. 20th, 1852.

IV.—4. Jane T. Collins, born 5 mo. 9th, 1853; married Samuel George Morton Maule, 10 mo. 3rd, 1876.

Issue:

V.—1. Margaret Collins Maule, born 2 mo. 6th, 1878.

V.—2. Alfred Collins Maule, born 11 mo. 6th, 1879.

V.—3. Frances Maule, born 1 mo. 28th, 1888.

IV.—5. Josephine Richards Collins, born 2 mo. 12th, 1858; married Joseph F. Page, Jr., 6 mo. 13th, 1878.

Issue:

V.—1. Charles Collins Page, born 4 mo. 11th, 1879.

V.—2. Edith Page, born 4 mo. 11th, 1880.

V.—3. Elizabeth Richards Page, born 11 mo. 17th, 1882.

V.—4. Joseph French Page (3rd), born 7 mo. 27th, 1885.

III.—6. Frederic Collins, born 1 mo. 21st, 1822; died 11 mo. 27th, 1892; married Letitia P. Dawson, daughter of Mordecai L. Dawson, 8 mo. 28th, 1844.

Issue:

IV.—1. Elizabeth Dawson Collins, born 1 mo. 23rd, 1847; married Charles F. Hulse, 6 mo. 3rd, 1869.

Issue:

V.—1. Letitia Collins Hulse, born 6 mo. 1st, 1870; married Samuel Bowman Wheeler, 4 mo. 28th, 1892.

V.—2. Margaret Morris Hulse, born 4 mo. 22nd, 1873.

IV.—2. Annie Morrison Collins, born 7 mo. 26th, 1849; married Morris Earle, 4 mo. 10th, 1890.

IV.—3. Frederic Collins, Jr., born 2 mo. 4th, 1868.

III.—7. Isaac Collins, Jr., born 5 mo. 2nd, 1824; married Elizabeth B. K. Earle, 12 mo. 9th, 1847.

Issue:

IV.—1. Thomas Earle Collins, born 7 mo. 3rd, 1849.

IV.—2. Catherine Earle Collins, born and died 9 mo. 12th, 1865.

III.—8. Theodore Collins, born 7 mo. 27th, 1826; died 9 mo. 4th, 1826.

III.—9. Margaret M. Collins, born 8 mo. 18th, 1829; married Oliver Keese Earle, of Worcester, Massachusetts, 6 mo. 1st, 1853; died 4 mo. 6th, 1863.

Issue:

IV.—1. Alfred Collins Earle, born 4 mo. 26th, 1854; died 5 mo. 4th, 1868.

IV.—2. Oliver Keese Earle, Jr., born 2 mo. 7th, 1857; married Emma Tyler Lacock, 1 mo. 2nd, 1879.

Issue:

V.—1. William K. Earle, born 12 mo. 3rd, 1879; died 12 mo. 8th, 1879.

V.—2. Mary A. B. Earle, born 1 mo. 29th, 1883; died 5 mo. 2nd, 1885.

V.—3. Margaret Morris Earle, born 6 mo. 9th, 1885.

V.—4. Walter Keese Earle, born 8 mo. 15th, 1886.

V.—5. Florence Mitchell Earle, born 12 mo. 20th, 1889.

IV.—3. Morris Earle, born 11 mo. 19th, 1859; married Annie Morrison Collins, 4 mo. 10th, 1890.

IV.—4. Margaret Collins Earle, born 3 mo. 31st, 1863.

III.—10. Percival Collins, born 12 mo. 19th, 1831; married Sarah A. Levick, 10 mo. 5th, 1856; died 5 mo. 7th, 1872.

Issue:

IV.—1. William L. Collins, born 7 mo. 1st, 1860; married Florence M. Crankshaw, 5 mo. 5th, 1886; died 6 mo. 12th, 1889.

IV.—2. Helen Morris Collins, born 5 mo. 14th, 1864; died 8 mo. 25th, 1864.

IV.—3. Margaret Morris Collins, born 1 mo. 19th, 1868; died 2 mo. 20th, 1873.

IV.—4. Elizabeth L. Collins, born 2 mo. 23rd, 1870; died 8 mo. 13th, 1870.

II.—11. Isaac Collins, son of Isaac and Rachel Collins, afterwards married Rebecca Singer, 1 mo. 28th, 1835, who died 4 mo. 30th, 1892. He died 1 mo. 15th, 1863.

Issue of Isaac and Rebecca Collins.

III.—1. Anna Collins, born 11 mo. 3rd, 1835; married John R. Taber, 9 mo. 26th, 1871.

Issue:

IV.—1. Marion Russell Taber, born 5 mo. 4th, 1875.

IV.—2. Josephine Collins Taber, born 5 mo. 16th, 1879.

III.—2. Stephen Grellet Collins, born 12 mo. 22nd, 1836; married Adelaide A. Knorr, 10 mo. 13th, 1860.

Issue:

IV.—1. Grellet Collins, born 1 mo. 20th, 1862; married Rebecca Woodside Newell, 4 mo. 23rd, 1885.

Issue:

V.—1. Dorothy Newell Collins, born 12 mo. 30th, 1887.

IV.—2. George Frederic Collins, born 11 mo. 2nd, 1863; married Jean L. Currie, 10 mo. 6th, 1886.

Issue:

V.—1. Ralph Wilberforce Collins, born 12 mo. 16th, 1887.

IV.—3. Percival Collins, born 2 mo. 19th, 1868; married Mary Helen Brown, 9 mo. 2nd, 1891.

IV.—4. Clarence Wilberforce Collins, born 6 mo. 3rd, 1869.

IV.—5. Adelaide A Collins, born 12 mo. 5th, 1870.

IV.—6. Isaac Collins, born 1 mo. 8th, 1874.

III.—3. Mary Forster Collins, born 3 mo. 1st, 1843; married James M. Walton, 11 mo. 28th, 1867.

Issue:

IV.—1. Elizabeth Walton, born 10 mo. 25th, 1868.

IV.—2. Ernest Forster Walton, born 4 mo. 5th, 1871.

II.—12. MARY COLLINS, daughter of Isaac and Rachel Collins, born 7 mo. 27th, 1789; married Isaac T. Longstreth, 10 mo. 27th, 1808; died 7 mo. 7th, 1865.

Issue:

III.—1. Mary Anna Longstreth, born 2 mo. 9th, 1811; died 8 mo. 15th, 1884.

III.—2. Susan Longstreth, born 1 mo. 4th, 1813.

III.—3. Henry Longstreth, born 7 mo. 11th, 1814.

III.—4. Elisabeth Longstreth, born 6 mo. 28th, 1817; married Israel Morris, 9 mo. 28th, 1839.

Issue:

IV.—1. Theodore H. Morris, born 10 mo. 10th, 1840; married Mary L. Paul, 9 mo. 3rd, 1863.

Issue :

V.—1. Elisabeth Morris, born 6 mo. 20th, 1864.
V.—2. Paul Jones Morris, born 9 mo. 14th, 1865; died 1 mo. 23rd, 1879.
V.—3. Israel Morris, born 1 mo. 23rd, 1867; died 2 mo. 13th, 1891.
V.—4. William Paul Morris, born 1 mo. 23rd, 1867; married Mary Bunting Sharp, 6 mo. 11th, 1889.

Issue :

VI.—1. Sydney Sharp Morris, born 3 mo. 24th, 1890.
V.—5. Ellen Morris, born 3 mo. 15th, 1868.
V.—6. Theodore Hollingsworth Morris, born 11 mo. 25th, 1869; died 2 mo. 15th, 1879.
V.—7. Samuel Paul Morris, born 11 mo. 23rd, 1871; died 2 mo. 9th, 1872.
V.—8. Sallie Paul Morris, born 2 mo. 3rd, 1873; died 2 mo. 16th, 1879.
V.—9. Anne Theodora Morris, born 7 mo. 21st, 1874.
V.—10. George Lownes Morris, born 11 mo. 25th, 1875.
V.—11. Evelyn Flower Morris, born 6 mo. 20th, 1877.
V.—12. Joseph Paul Morris, born 1 mo. 1st, 1879.
V.—13. Charles Christopher Morris, born 6 mo. 30th, 1882.
V.—14. Harold Hollingsworth Morris, born 1 mo. 16th, 1884.
V.—15. Jacqueline Pascal Morris, born 4 mo. 12th, 1886.
V.—16. Katharine Wistar Morris, born 9 mo. 25th, 1887.

IV.—2. Frederick Wistar Morris, born 3 mo. 18th, 1842; married Elizabeth F. Paul, 9 mo. 3rd, 1866.

Issue :

V.—1. Frederick Wistar Morris, born 5 mo. 26th, 1867.
V.—2. Margaret Elizabeth Morris, born 2 mo. 9th, 1870.
V.—3. Marian Longstreth Morris, born 11 mo. 9th, 1872.
V.—4. Samuel Wheeler Morris, born 1 mo. 16th, 1874.
V.—5. John Paul Morris, born 9 mo. 16th, 1876.
V.—6. Dorothea Hollingsworth Morris, born 9 mo. 22nd, 1879.

V.—7. Pauline Flower Morris, born 12 mo. 21st, 1880.

IV.—3. Anna Morris, born 11 mo. 20th, 1844.

IV.—4. William Henry Morris, born 3 mo. 25th, 1846; married Sallie W. Paul, 12 mo. 3rd, 1868.

Issue:

V.—1. Richard Jones Morris, born 9 mo. 2nd, 1869.

V.—2. Mary Paul Morris, born 4 mo. 22nd, 1871; married Paschall Hollingsworth Morris, 9 mo. 17th, 1890.

Issue:

VI.—1. Sallie Hollingsworth Morris, born 6 mo. 8th, 1891.

V.—3. Alfred Paul Morris, born 9 mo. 2nd, 1875.

V.—4. Arthur W. Morris, born 8 mo. 24th, 1877; died 4 mo. 25th, 1878.

V.—5. Francis Bolton Morris, born 4 mo. 9th, 1885.

V.—6. Reginald Hollingsworth Morris, born 6 mo. 14th, 1887.

III.—5. William Collins Longstreth, born 3 mo. 12th, 1821; married Abby Ann Taylor, 11 mo. 16th, 1848; died 4 mo. 25th, 1881.

Issue:

IV.—1. Benjamin Taylor Longstreth, born 8 mo. 16th, 1849; married Frances Haldeman, 4 mo. 29th, 1885, who died 3 mo. 24th, 1888.

Issue:

V.—1. Thomas Morris Longstreth, born 2 mo. 17th, 1886.

V.—2. Frances H. Longstreth, born and died 3 mo. 24th, 1888.

IV.—1. Benjamin Taylor Longstreth married Sara Gibson Haldeman (his second wife), 11 mo. 14th, 1889.

Issue:

V.—1. Walter Wood Longstreth, born 10 mo. 6th, 1890.

IV.—2. Thomas Kimber Longstreth, born 8 mo. 30th, 1851; married Lucy Branson, 10 mo. 27th, 1880; died 3 mo. 3rd, 1883.

Issue:

V.—1. William Collins Longstreth, born 3 mo. 13th, 1882.

IV.—3. William Morris Longstreth, born 7 mo. 7th, 1853; married Elizabeth Inskeep Church, 10 mo. 17th, 1888.

Issue:

V.—1. Dorothy Longstreth, born 6 mo. 20th, 1890.

V.—2. William Church Longstreth, born 12 mo. 16th, 1891.

IV.—4. Henry Longstreth, born 6 mo. 27th, 1855; married Emma V. Smith, 6 mo. 1st, 1887.

Issue:

V.—1. Henry Longstreth, born 11 mo. 26th, 1888.

V.—2. Grellet Longstreth, born 6 mo. 13th, 1890.

V.—3. Margaret Longstreth, born 3 mo. 1st, 1892.

IV.—5. Charles Albert Longstreth, born 5 mo. 20th, 1857; married Ellen Warder Pearsall, 11 mo. 4th, 1885.

IV.—6. Mary Longstreth, born 6 mo. 20th, 1859; married George E. Shoemaker, M.D., 10 mo. 15th, 1889.

Issue:

V.—1. Marian Taylor Shoemaker, born 3 mo. 21st, 1891.

IV.—7. Sara Morris Longstreth, born 2 mo. 4th, 1865.

IV.—8. Anna Longstreth, born 2 mo. 9th, 1868; died 7 mo. 10th, 1868.

IV.—9. Edward Rhoads Longstreth, born 1 mo. 31st, 1871.

II.—13. STACY BUDD COLLINS, born 1 mo. 19th, 1791; married Mary E. Dudley, 10 mo. 11th, 1821. He died 6 mo. 23rd, 1873.

Issue:

III.—1. Emma Dudley Collins, born 5 mo. 23rd, 1823; died 6 mo. 18th, 1842.

III.—2. Anna Dudley Collins, born 6 mo. 25th, 1825; died 1 mo. 7th, 1834.

III.—3. Cornelia Collins, born 7 mo. 7th, 1827; married William H. Hussey, 4 mo. 16th, 1851.

Issue :

IV.—1. Mary Hussey, born 7 mo. 31st, 1853.

IV.—2. Frederic Hussey, born 6 mo. 14th, 1856.

IV.—3. George B. Hussey, born 3 mo. 10th, 1863.

III.—4. Mary Stacy Collins, born 11 mo. 2nd, 1829; married John Murray, Jr., 10 mo. 2nd, 1862; died 4 mo. 1st, 1875.

Issue :

IV.—1. John Murray, Jr., born 11 mo. 27th, 1865; married Gertrude Etchison.

III.—5. Sarah Collins, born 9 mo. 14th, 1831; married Joshua H. Worthington, M.D., 11 mo. 23rd, 1876.

III.—6. Theodore Collins, born 9 mo. 27th, 1833; died 12 mo. 28th, 1835.

III.—7. Edward Dudley Collins, born 10 mo. 15th, 1836; died 1 mo. 1st, 1838.

II.—13. Stacy Budd Collins married Hannah West Jenks (second wife), 11 mo. 2nd, 1843, and died 6 mo. 23rd, 1873.

Issue :

III.—1. Stacy Budd Collins, Jr., born 8 mo. 8th, 1847; married Mary Tyson, 12 mo. 6th, 1883.

III.—2. Gertrude Collins, born 9 mo. 15th, 1849.

II.—14. Joseph Budd Collins, born 1 mo. 30th, 1794; married Sarah Minturn, 10 mo. 2nd, 1822; died 9 mo. 16th, 1867.

Issue :

III.—1. Mary Minturn Collins, born 10 mo. 2nd, 1823.

III.—2. Caroline Minturn Collins, born 12 mo. 5th, 1826; died 12 mo. 26th, 1826.

III.—3. Ellen Collins, born 2 mo. 15th, 1829.

III.—4. Margaret Collins, born 7 mo. 16th, 1832.

APPENDIX.

FREDERIC COLLINS.

APPENDIX.

FREDERIC COLLINS.

FREDERIC COLLINS, son of Isaac 2d and Margaret Morris Collins, was born in New York City, January 21, 1822. At this time his father was engaged in the book-publishing business, which was afterwards purchased by the well-known firm of Harper Brothers, former employés of the house.

In accordance with a resolve made early in his business life, having acquired a competence which he deemed sufficient to provide a comfortable home and good education for his children, Isaac Collins retired from business at the early age of thirty-four years, and devoted the rest of his life to benevolent and charitable work. His many business friends were surprised at his action, and advised him to continue in a business which was lucrative; but he held to his original purpose, knowing that the inheritance of a large fortune might in no way be a blessing to his sons, but might curb their ambition. His course proved to be a wise one in its influence upon his children, and his example was closely followed by his son Frederic, as well as by his other sons, who have given much of their time and money to charitable work of many kinds. Margaret Morris, the mother of Frederic Collins, was the daughter of Dr. John Morris and Abigail Dorsey. She was left an orphan at a very early age by the sudden death from yellow fever of both her parents in 1793. Her grandmother, Margaret Morris, consequently took care of her and brought her up. This noted old lady, a descendant of Thomas Lloyd, one of the early governors of Pennsylvania, was living in Burlington, New Jersey, where, during the Colonial and Revolutionary days, she entertained many of the celebrated men of the day, including Washington and La Fayette. She was a woman of education and great refinement, as may be seen from her many letters and diary written during the Revolution, which have been very properly preserved in the book of the Hill Family. In the words of John Jay Smith, in his introduction to the book of the Hill Family, "the preservation of such records is due, as a tribute to the memory of the just, and may serve as an incentive to honorable and virtuous conduct; for, while it is a false and absurd vanity which strives to deck itself in plumes borrowed from the past, the desire to emulate a noble example, which has descended to us as an inheritance, is worthy of all fame."

The boyhood of Frederic Collins was spent partly in New York, where, at a very early age, he was placed by his father in the public school in Crosby Street, through the desire of the latter to show by his own example that he approved the new system which he had been largely instrumental in establishing. The family lived in Broome Street, east of Crosby Street, and afterwards removed to a house of three stories on the east side of Broadway, the only one of its kind where it was located, below Houston Street. It was in this house that Frederic Collins was wont to relate that people flocked to see a coal fire, or, as they styled it, "to see stone burn," as his father was the first to use anthracite coal in New York.

On account of the delicate health of his mother, the family moved, in the spring of 1828, to Philadelphia, where they lived first in a rented house on the south side of Arch Street, below Twelfth. Soon afterwards they moved to a new house built by his father on the north side of Filbert Street, above Twelfth, where the brightest hours of his boyhood were passed, and which he never tired of narrating. It was there that they had a room in the upper part of the house devoted to the amusement of the boys when they met to study their lessons and play upon their musical instruments, at which times they were frequently joined by their father, who would accompany them on the flute; for, notwithstanding that he wore a plain coat, he believed that by making his home attractive to his children he would not only make them happy, but also gain their companionship and confidence.

When thirteen years old Frederic Collins entered Haverford School, now a college, and on account of his youth found much difficulty in performing the hard tasks required, but finally he graduated with honor. Among his acquaintances and classmates were Thomas P. Cope, Francis R. Cope, Henry Hartshorne, and his cousin, Lloyd P. Smith, who were afterwards his life-long friends.

After graduation he entered business as a clerk for the firm of Philip B. Chase & Co., commission dry-goods merchants, where he showed such ability that he was admitted to partnership before he became of age.

On the 28th of August, 1844, he married Letitia Poultney Dawson, daughter of Mordecai Lewis and Elizabeth Poultney Dawson.

His first business venture proving unsuccessful, he entered the firm of M. L. Dawson & Co., brewers, and on the retirement of his father-in-law, the firm of Poultney, Collins & Massey was formed, in which he proved himself a most capable business-man, pushing the business with untiring energy, and through travel, study, and experiments placed himself in the foremost ranks of his trade in America.

Withdrawing from this firm, he entered the stock brokerage business with Mr. Samuel Huston, but soon went back at the solicitation of Mr. William Massey, and formed the partnership of Massey, Collins & Co., where he remained until 1866 in active business with great success. Through the extended connections and increased capital they were large purchasers of grain, both in the East and West, so that he became very well known and received many flattering and advantageous offers to enter business in New York, especially from some of the largest houses.

Early in 1864 he went, in company with his cousin, Lloyd P. Smith, on a commission to East Tennessee, for the purpose of relieving the sufferings of the loyal people of that region, who had been sorely pressed by the rebels of the South. Contributions of provisions and money to the amount of two hundred and fifty thousand dollars having been collected through the labors of the Philadelphia authorities under Colonel N. G. Taylor, of Knoxville, East Tennessee, and also from New England under Edward Everett, Frederic Collins and Lloyd P. Smith went to Cincinnati, where they arranged the necessary details for purchasing and forwarding supplies. From Cincinnati they were passed through to Knoxville, receiving every assistance from the army officers, being furnished with a letter of introduction and commendation from the Assistant Secretary of War, C. A. Dana.*

---

* "WAR DEPARTMENT, WASHINGTON CITY, March 2, 1864

"GENERAL,—An association for the relief of those citizens of East Tennessee who have been reduced to destitution by the events of the war has been formed

Another incident worth relating, to demonstrate the readiness with which he was always acting in response to the request of others upon his time, occurred while on a trip to Washington, when he visited the camp of a Philadelphia regiment. The men were just from home, and impatiently waiting for a summons to advance to the front. Mr. Collins asked what he could do to make them more comfortable, and they said, "Send us down a band." He returned to Philadelphia that night, and the next day, on his way down town from his home at 1918 Spruce Street, he stopped at the house of his father-in-law and asked him for a check for one hundred dollars "for a good cause," which was readily given, and getting one of a like amount from his own firm, he went directly to the Exchange and raised the balance of six hundred dollars, and sent the band down the same day, to the great gratification of the homesick boys in camp.

Such was his position in his business and the respect in which he was held, that he was requested to engage two other men, and with these men to proceed to Europe and collect information concerning the excise tax laws of the various beer-drinking communities, in order that a memorial could be presented to the Commissioners to be appointed by the Secretary of the United States Treasury.

In April, 1865, he went with Mr. M. P. Read, of New York, and Mr. Frederic Lauer, of Reading, Pennsylvania, to Europe, where they made a careful study of the subject, and on their return presented their report, which, with the investigation that followed, re-

---

in Philadelphia, and a considerable sum has been raised to procure supplies. The association has appointed as its Commissioners for the distribution of these supplies Messrs. Frederic Collins, Colonel N. G. Taylor, and Lloyd P. Smith. I beg to commend them to your kindness, and to request that you will render them any assistance which may be in your power. They should have free transportation for themselves, their agents, and supplies which they desire to distribute, upon all government railroads and chartered vessels."

The above letter bears the following endorsement:

"This letter will serve to introduce the bearers to General Schofield or any other commanding officers to whom they may have occasion to apply, besides General Grant.

"C. A. DANA,

"*Assistant Secretary of War.*"

(*Vide* p. 38.) **Report to the contributors to the Pennsylvania Relief Association for East Tennessee.** L. P. SMITH.

lieved the manufacturing communities from the difficulties which had so heavily oppressed them.

During the last few years of his business life the character of the trade essentially changed, so that the associations and methods became extremely distasteful to him, and he withdrew from business and with his wife and two daughters went to Europe, where they remained for nearly a year. Upon his return from Europe he continued in the presidency of the McKean and Elk Land and Improvement Company, but withdrew in 1868. In 1869 he was elected a member of the Board of the House of Refuge, which position he retained for the rest of his life.

His interest in business matters and his active mind naturally led him back into business, which he again entered with William Elliot, forming the banking concern of Elliot, Collins & Co., and remaining in it until 1873.

In accordance with the example of his father, and by his own inclination, he withdrew from business and devoted himself to charitable and benevolent work in many public and private ways. He had been a member of the Board of the House of Refuge since 1869, but he now entered upon the work in the same active manner in which he had previously carried on his business enterprises. He was Secretary of the Board from 1870 to 1878, Vice-President from 1878 to 1885, and President from 1885 to the day of his death, November 27, 1892.

From 1878 he kept a journal in which he jotted down the everyday happenings of his work in the House of Refuge and his thoughts on matters private and public, and throughout its pages there runs a deep current of religious feeling which guided his every act.

He was a member of the religious Society of Friends, being the oldest member of Twelfth Street Meeting.

In his work at the House of Refuge he believed that the principles of guidance should be those of reformation rather than of punishment, and the carrying out of these principles he considered only possible by the cottage system, as the congregate system required more the manner of prison life.

To carry out his views, obtained by persistent study and travel, required never-ending work, and he was engaged day and night. Finally, after several unsuccessful appeals had been made to the Legislature to buy the property occupied in the city, and after his colleagues had given up all hope, he laid out a course of action which was crowned with success. He succeeded in raising seven hundred thousand dollars, and lived to see it carefully expended under his own direction,—to see the six hundred boys transferred, and the new institution under a most competent superintendent whom he had very carefully selected after having visited many institutions in New England and the West.

On account of his varied experience he was much sought after, and received many offers of positions of trust, accepting many such and without any remuneration. He was a director of the Provident Life and Trust Company, the Western National Bank, and the Western Saving Fund. His business training enabled him to treat the work of charity in a business way rather than as one of mere sentiment. He was full of versatility and tact, comprehending at once with clear judgment the proper fitness of things, and with an indomitable will added to a wonderfully strong constitution, he was an acknowledged leader in all he attempted.

Such was the life of Frederic Collins, filled with a noble desire to do good in the world, and, what was better, constantly doing it. His enjoyments were those of a happy home and a host of life-long friends, to whom his warm-hearted hospitality was ever extended.

In 1892, accompanied by his friends, Mr. James V. Watson and Mr. William B. Rogers, he went to Chicago to attend the opening ceremonies of the Columbian Exhibition, and on his return he felt so rejuvenated and refreshed that he again entered upon his work unsparingly. He attempted more than his strength would bear, as, after a few days' illness, he succumbed to a sudden attack of pneumonia on November 27, 1892.

There could not be a more fitting tribute to his memory than the resolutions adopted by the contributors to the House of Refuge, as they show how highly he was prized as a friend and guide in the chosen work of his life. Many men have been more renowned than Frederic Collins, but none have been more beloved for noble deeds and sacrifices for the good of others.

"The House of Refuge is a vast power for good, and as its influence shall be more widely disseminated, it must become a still greater force in restoring the fallen to rectitude and of conferring happiness upon those who know but little of the delights of the law-abiding and the virtuous. May heaven's richest blessing rest upon our future labor in this glorious cause.

"At the annual meeting of the contributors to the House of Refuge, held January 11, 1893, the following preamble and resolutions were adopted:

"'WHEREAS, This meeting has learned with great sorrow the sad news of the death of Frederic Collins, President of the institution, on November 27, 1892.

"'*Resolved*, That the contributors desire to place on record their earnest sense of the serious loss to the House of Refuge of their President, who for over twenty-three years devoted his time and labor to its needs and interests. Thorough in administration, able and energetic, he was a pioneer in every reform in its management. His interest in the House of Refuge was inherited from his father, the late Isaac Collins, who, after assisting in the establishment of the New York House of Refuge, devoted himself to that in Philadelphia, and brought up his sons so as to fit them to carry on and enlarge and improve the work of reforming the children intrusted to its care. The family have dedicated one of its buildings to his memory, and the unselfish services of his sons to the House of Refuge have made their names, as well as his own, part of its long record of usefulness. Every child, every officer, and every manager with whom Frederic Collins was brought in contact will bear grateful remembrance of his constant kindness, tender solicitude, and generous sympathy. His interest in its inmates extended long beyond their stay, and he was always ready to give them useful advice and substantial help. As the official representative of the House of Refuge with the State, the city, the judiciary, and the public, his thorough knowledge of the institution and its needs, his constant courtesy, his unfailing zeal, made him invaluable. His loss will indeed long be felt as irreparable. His active employment in many responsible positions of both public and private trust, his large business experience, his administrative capacity, made him a leading citizen; but amidst the pressure of all his cares and duties he was always mindful of the claims and needs of the House of Refuge, and the last years of his life were spent in perfecting the great task of its transfer from a prison-like city institution to its present cottage homes in the midst of a great farm.

"'*Resolved*, That the Board of Managers be requested in due season to endeavor to adopt some form of memorial which shall suitably perpetuate his name by a building at the House of Refuge at Glen Mills, such as will at all times serve to keep alive the recollection of his great and successful efforts on its behalf, and in this plan invite the co-operation of all those who knew and loved and honored him for his great public spirit and his many personal virtues.'"

MARY ANNA LONGSTRETH.

Mary Anna Longstreth, eldest daughter of Isaac T. and Mary Longstreth, so well known and esteemed throughout the city of Philadelphia by its many teachers and prominent citizens, was born February 9, 1811, and began her education at the age of five years. When eight years old she commenced the study of Latin, and in order to assist her, her worthy aunt, Anna S. Collins, began the study at the same time. Dr. J. P. Price, afterwards a missionary to Burmah, was engaged to teach her Latin, as in 1819 there was no school in the city where girls could be taught Latin and Greek. The first five hundred dollars that could be spared from her earnings were given for a Dr. Price scholarship. "Honor the Lord with thy substance" was the law of her life.

Before she was twelve years old she had read every word of Virgil, and was so well acquainted with the language that she was engaged as assistant classical teacher in John Brewer's school when only thirteen years of age. These years of early girlhood were full of quiet happiness. Her private journal notes her lively gratitude to her heavenly Father for health, happiness, and ability to fulfil her duties as a teacher and in the family.

In 1829 she and her sister Susan, when eighteen and sixteen years of age respectively, opened a school at No. 3 North Eleventh Street. Though small at first, in Ninth month, 1830, it numbered fourteen pupils. Antony Bolmar was employed as French teacher, but Mr. Gardell succeeded him in 1833, remaining till its close in 1877. One of their earliest scholars writes thus: "Three happy years I passed under the care of these admirable women, and have since had the privilege of their friendship and continued sympathy. Mine was the first of the many marriages of their pupils that they attended, and I still cherish the picture of the humming-bird, the orange-blossoms, and the appropriate verses presented at that time."

Anxious to improve themselves, the sisters took lessons in drawing and perspective, and attended lectures on natural philosophy, chemistry, etc.

In the summer of 1835 they made a visit to Niagara, being greatly invigorated by it. In January, 1836, Mary Anna writes, "We have now an assemblage of the most amiable and interesting pupils we have ever had." In the autumn the school was removed to more commodious quarters in Cherry Street, where it was continued the next twenty-one years. In 1838 the hall on Sixth Street where the Women's Abolition Society was holding its convention was set on fire and destroyed. They then adjourned to the second story of the house where the sisters held their school. The mob determined to burn it also, but, through the kind and zealous efforts of Mordecai L. Dawson and others, it dispersed without doing any injury.

The next four or five years the school prospered greatly. In 1839 the youngest sister, Elizabeth, who had for several years taken part in the teaching, was married to Israel Morris. In the financial troubles of 1842 some of the schools in the city were entirely broken up, and theirs was greatly reduced in number on this account for two years, but was carried on most pleasantly and satisfactorily. Very often did the sisters visit Greenway, the delightful rural home of their ever-kind aunt, Susan Longstreth.

In 1844–45 prosperity returned, and in 1847–48 a hundred applicants were necessarily refused. In March, 1849, Mary Anna writes, "I have had an exceedingly busy winter, the most laborious, I think, I have ever had. Twenty-two of our pupils are over sixteen years of age, and are capable of accomplishing a great amount of study and writing, so that their translations, exercises, etc., have given me a great deal of work at home. But I have been remarkably favored with health. It has been my best winter in that respect for years." The same year her faithful sister and assistant, Susan, found it necessary to give up her arduous labors for a more domestic life, yet still aided in making out reports of lessons and conduct.

Having been overtasked for several years, the two sisters, with a party of friends and relatives, went to England, Scotland, France, Germany, Switzerland, and Italy, visiting many friends in England, and deriving great enjoyment from the varied scenery of their extended route and all the incidents of the journey. After a season of comparative rest, on coming back the school was again opened on Cherry Street, but a few years later, finding the premises too small, it was removed to the corner of Filbert and Juniper Streets, to begin in January, 1858. To obviate the necessity of the girls going out to buy luncheon of some pastry cook, Mary Anna engaged a respectable colored woman to prepare wholesome biscuits, tarts, and cakes for them at recess. The fourth story of the large building was used as a gymnasium.

The school now numbered ninety pupils, with twenty-seven teachers, only six of them being employed all the time; but Mary Anna feeling the need of a longer rest than the ordinary vacation, joined her brother and sister Morris in a second visit to Europe, following the route taken before, except that more time was given to Holland and a brief visit paid to Rome. They returned in November.

In 1867, the school property being wanted for the new Masonic Temple, the school was removed to Merrick Street, facing the four Penn squares, where the great pile of white marble—Public Buildings—now rises.

After fifty years of successful teaching and training hundreds of pupils, on the 20th of June, 1877, her school life closed. A most affectionate letter of resignation had been printed and distributed to all her scholars, in response to which "letters, notes, and messages, some of sympathy, some of congratulation, all of affection, came pouring in."

But her labors of love and sympathy did not end with her school career. For a time she visited the prisoners in the Penitentiary; she was one of the corporators of the Medical College for Women, and also a manager of the Woman's Hospital. But the most absorbing interest of all her later years was the school at Hampton, Virginia. In this she took the most delight, and lavished upon it every means at her command. A letter from General S. C. Armstrong, appealing to the Freedmen's Aid Society, being shown to her, she encouraged her scholars to bring their weekly contributions, amounting in one year to two hundred dollars, which work was continued until one scholarship was paid for, to which she added another.

For nine years she was an always-expected and never-failing guest at every anniversary of the institution. Her donations were continual. Bible lessons, historical charts, illuminated texts, philosophical apparatus, books, tracts, engravings, drawing models, pencils, dolls, aprons, calico dresses, coats, jackets, hats and hoods, quilts and blankets, beads, toys, Noah's arks, thimbles, tools, etc., filled their parlors at times, in Filbert Street, ready for packing and shipment. Not the least valuable were her kind, sympathetic, Christian letters to the teachers and pupils at Hampton, among them being twenty colored ones.

In a letter to General Armstrong, dated September 11, 1876, she says, "While I have the ability, and it is day with me, I desire to work. I know not how soon the night may come. At the same time I do not intend to shorten the day by overtaxing my strength contrary to the laws of Him who makes the body as well as the soul." On one occasion she said to a Hampton teacher, "I have often thought that if I should be allowed by the dear Lord to choose my occupation in heaven, I should choose to teach." Many there are who would echo that teacher's answer, "Then I hope I may be in your class there." The ever-present thought of Mary Anna Longstreth, at Hampton, will be, "Our beloved friend is present with us as an inspiration to better living and as a reminder of the blessedness of using for others what has been given to us. Surely her name and face will be a heavenly influence, like that of a guardian angel, helping all who pass within these walls."

In 1884 the three sisters spent six weeks at Cape May, hoping that the fine air from the beach and the perfect quiet would restore the failing health and strength of the beloved invalid; but, by the advice of her physician, early in August she was taken back to her own home. On the 14th, at 6 P.M., new symptoms appearing, the doctor was immediately sent for, but before he could reach the bedside she was unconscious. At four o'clock next morning her breathing ceased, most of the intervening hours having been passed in gentle slumber. Her countenance, beautiful in death, seemed to bear witness to the two hundred who gathered at the funeral that the sting of death had been taken away and the victory gained through our Lord Jesus Christ.

"Blessed are the dead which die in the Lord: . . . Yea, saith the Spirit, that they may rest from their labours; and their works do follow them."—REV. xiv. 13.

WILLIAM C. LONGSTRETH.

William C. Longstreth, son of Isaac T. and Mary Longstreth, was born on the 12th of Third month, 1821. His mental faculties were early developed. He began the study of Latin at six years of age and read Virgil at eight. When twelve years old he entered Haverford School, and graduated with honor in 1838, being a member of one of the earlier classes receiving diplomas.

In after-years he became a manager of the institution. In 1839 and 1840 he learned every kind of farm work, particularly that pertaining to a dairy. In 1842 he bought Locust Grove, of sixty acres, in Springfield, Delaware County, cultivating it very assiduously. In the fall of 1848 he married Ably Ann Taylor, whose parents, Benjamin and Sarah Taylor, lived near Mount Holly, New Jersey. It was a union of congenial hearts, divinely blessed and most happy in the conjugal relation. Five children were born to them on that place. But an injury caused by a fall in the barn made it improper for William to do hard work, and he accepted a situation in the Williamsport and Elmira Railroad Company as Secretary and Treasurer. He then sold Locust Grove and removed to the Greenway farm, near Philadelphia. Here he and his wife established the Greenway Sabbath-School, which increased rapidly, and has always been a blessing to the neighborhood. As soon as the children were old enough they all took part in it.

About this time the Young Men's Christian Association established prayer-meetings throughout the city, and one was opened at the house where the Sabbath-School was held. Many will give thanks through all eternity for this opportunity of grace.

Two daughters and one son were added to the family at Greenway. All the children were taught implicit obedience before they were three months old, and the greatest harmony always subsisted between them and their beloved parents in the fear and service of the Lord.

For nine years the family occupied the old house at Greenway, and then he built the present home (1890), Ingleside, in order to enjoy larger accommodations.

Having served the Williamsport and Elmira Railroad Company with great energy and business talents, he was made the First Vice-

President of the Provident Life and Trust Company, where his uniform courtesy and suavity of manner made him a general favorite. At home he was the life of the family, and in conversation none could excel him. In early life not only were his views of Christian truth remarkably correct, but he had given his heart to the Saviour. For the last twenty-two years of his life he accepted the Gospel offers of salvation still more heartily than ever before, and rejoiced in the belief that he was accepted of the Lord and safe in Him. For fifteen years his fellow-members of Darby Meeting had the privilege of hearing from his lips the presentation of the necessity of making an entire surrender to the truth as it is in Christ Jesus our Lord. His ministry attracted many to the meeting, and was fully sanctioned by his friends, both at home and abroad.

With the assistance of relatives and friends he erected a large and commodious edifice for the Greenway Sabbath-School, Mothers' Meetings, Sewing-School, and Temperance Work. He also took a warm interest in Friends' First-Day School Conference from its beginning, being Chairman of the Executive Committee to the close of his life.

In the summer of 1880, while at Newport, he took cold, and ever afterwards suffered attacks of pain occasionally, but not until First month of 1881 was he kept at home. A short visit to Old Point Comfort, Virginia, Second month 19th, was undertaken, but proved of no benefit. So gradual was his decline during the last six weeks of his life that his family could hardly realize that he was approaching the valley of the shadow of death. When they found that this was the case, they felt without the slightest doubt that his Saviour was with him every step of the way, leading him gently and safely to his home in heaven to be forever with the Lord.

He entered into rest on the 25th of Fourth month, 1881, in the sixty-first year of his age.

A large company of relatives and friends assembled the day of burial, and not a few ministers bore witness to the lovely character of the departed one, his Christian graces, consecration to his Saviour, and the work which, through divine favor and help, he had done in this life.

The following words from a letter of sympathy of President Thomas Chase, of Haverford, are as true as appropriate: "No man that I ever knew exemplified more fully in his domestic life the beauty of holiness. He was a model of every Christian grace, and indeed, 'a living epistle.' Wherever he went he bore by word and deed an unfailing testimony for his Lord and Master, and commended the doctrine he professed by his constant courtesy, cheerfulness, and kindliness. He carried sunshine with him, and his presence was a continual benediction."

Testimonial of the Provident Life and Trust Company.

"PHILADELPHIA, Fourth month 27, 1881.

"At a special meeting of the Directors of the Company, held this day, the following minute was adopted:

"'William C. Longstreth, the Vice-President of the Company, having been removed by death, the Board of Directors desire to place upon record their sense of his value as an associate and his faithful services as an official. He has been connected with the management since its foundation, and has been the second officer of the Company for fourteen years. During this long period his singular urbanity, combined with an unswerving integrity and large experience, rendered him a most efficient and valuable aid in the transaction of its business.

"The actions of the just
Smell sweet and blossom in the dust."

We sincerely mourn his removal, and tender to his bereaved widow and family our heart-felt sympathy in their irreparable loss.'

"On behalf of the Board,
"SAMUEL R. SHIPLEY, *President.*"

THE COLLINS COAT OF ARMS.

ISAAC COLLINS, in a letter addressed to Thomas Stewardson, alludes to a report of his having an uncle named William, and another who followed the sea and became captain or commander of a vessel trading to New York.

From the following correspondence it seems probable that the said William had in his possession a Collins coat of arms.

"HADDONFIELD, N. J., August 29, 1872.

"My wife was a daughter of Susan Whitton Sprague, daughter of Sarah Collins, who was a daughter of Joseph Collins, son of Captain William Collins, who settled somewhere in what was then Massachusetts, and whose family residing in

COAT OF ARMS

Maine had the original coat of arms, a copy of which is now in our possession. Joseph Collins married a Miss Bradbury, who lived in Portland, Maine, then Falmouth, when it was burned by the British. The family records may have been destroyed on that occasion.

"William Collins, the supposed brother of Charles Collins (uncle of Isaac), came from England about the same time as the latter, and settled in New England. His only son married Miss Bradbury as stated, and afterwards removed to New Gloucester, Maine. He had ten children, several of whom were seafaring men. One of them, Daniel, lived at that place, and the Collins Coat of Arms was left to him by his father, but it was afterwards transferred to another brother named James, of Gardiner, Maine. After his death it came into the possession of Captain Jason Collins, of that town, who has been engaged as engineer or commander of one of the steamers of the Boston and Kennebec line for more than fifty years.

"Signed, HENRY T. CLAY."

"STEAMER KENNEBEC, GARDINER, October 15, 1892.

"To JOHN COLLINS,—Yours of the 8th of October, addressed to Henry T. Clay, received this day, asking for information regarding the Collins family. I have always understood that there were three branches, one in Philadelphia, one in Cape Cod, Massachusetts, and one in Maine. The one in Maine I am a descendant of. They were formerly in the town of Gloucester. My grandfather's name was Joseph. He had several brothers, one of whom followed the sea. E. K. Collins, of New York, of the Collins line of steamers, was of the Cape Cod family. I send you a photograph of the Coat of Arms in my possession. We have always supposed that we were of Scotch descent, as the thistle in the Coat of Arms would indicate. The family here in Maine are all very large men, many of them over six feet in height, and but very few under six feet.

"JASON COLLINS."

Further information respecting William Collins may be obtained at some future time, and the relationship to Isaac Collins established. For this reason alone is the subject introduced in connection with the biography.

THE HAMMOND FAMILY.

I.—DANIEL HAMMOND, born in England; came over to America with other immigrants. He married Mary Elliot, of Nottingham, Pennsylvania.

Issue:

II.—1. Elizabeth.

II.—2. John married (first) Deborah Dicks, of Chester County, Pennsylvania.

Issue:

III.—1. Sarah Hammond married William Griffith.

Issue:

IV.—1. Thomas.

IV.—2. Nathan.

III.—2. Elizabeth Hammond married John Wright.

Issue:

IV.—1. Deborah.

IV.—2. Betsy.

IV.—3. Ruth.

IV.—4. Sally.

III.—3. Isaac Hammond.

III.—4. Nathan Hammond married Rachel Blackburn.

Issue:

IV.—1. Deborah.

IV.—2. Sarah.

IV.—3. John.

III.—5. James.

III.—6. John.

III.—7. Mary.

III.—8. Esther.

III.—9. Tamar.

II.—3. Sarah Hammond married Charles Collins.

Issue:

III.—1. Elizabeth.

III.—2. Isaac married Rachel Budd.

THE STACY FAMILY.

I.—Mahlon Stacy came from England in 1678, and left one son, named Mahlon, who married Sarah Bainbridge.

Issue:

II.—1. Mary Stacy married Reuben Pounal.

II.—2. Sarah Stacy married Joseph Kirkbride.

Issue:

III.—1. Mahlon Kirkbride.

II.—3. Rebecca Stacy married Joshua Wright.

Issue:

III.—1. Joshua.

III.—2. Nathan.

III.—3. Mahlon.

III.—4. David married —— ——.

Issue:

IV.—1. Robert.

IV.—2. Theodosia.

IV.—3. Joshua (deceased).

IV.—4. David.

IV.—5. Aaron.

IV.—6. Moses.

IV.—7. Sarah.

IV.—8. Elizabeth.

IV.—9. Joshua.

II.—4. Elizabeth Stacy married Amos Janney, and left children.

II.—5. Ruth Stacy married William Beakes.

Issue:

III.—1. Sarah Beakes married Thomas Potts. (He was the father of Stacy Potts, mayor of Trenton, whose children were, by his first wife, Mary, Sarah, Elizabeth, and William; by his second wife, Anna, Rebecca, and Joseph.)

III.—2. Stacy Beakes.

III.—3. Nathan Beakes.

II.—5. Ruth Stacy married (secondly) Samuel Atkinson.

Issue:

III.—1. Elizabeth.
III.—2. Ruth.
III.—3. Stacy.
III.—4. William.
III.—5. Rebecca.
III.—6. Ann.
III.—7. Mary.
III.—8. Samuel.
III.—9. Sarah.
III.—10. Mahlon.
III.—11. Beulah.
III.—12. Thomas Atkinson married Susanna Shinn.

Issue:

IV.—1. Martha.
IV.—2. William.
IV.—3. John.

II.—6. Rebecca married Thomas Budd.

Issue:

III.—1. Stacy.
III.—2. Elizabeth.
III.—3. Joseph.
III.—4. Rachel, who married Isaac Collins.

SAMUEL GEORGE MORTON.

Samuel George Morton, naturalist, anatomist, ethnologist, and physician, was descended from a highly-connected family in Clonmel, Ireland. His father, George Morton, came to America in 1773, and engaged in mercantile pursuits, and later was appointed Assistant Commissary of Issues. He married Jane, daughter of John and Margaret Cummings, in 1785, and died in Philadelphia, July 28, 1799, of yellow fever.

Samuel George Morton, who was born in Philadelphia, January 26, 1799, early evinced a passionate fondness for books and a thirst

Samuel George Morton

for knowledge, and combined with these a habit of persevering and methodical industry. He graduated at the University of Pennsylvania in March, 1820, and in October of the same year entered the University of Edinburgh. Having presented a thesis in Latin, "De Corporis Dolore," the diploma of the institution was conferred upon him in August, 1823. He returned to America in 1824, commenced the practice of medicine in 1826, and on October 23, 1827, he married Rebecca Grellet, daughter of Robert and Elizabeth Pearsall, members of the Society of Friends.

His first scientific essay, entitled "Observations on Cornine, a New Alkaloid," was published in the *Medical and Physical Journal* for 1825–26. In 1827 he communicated to the Academy of Natural Sciences an "Analysis of Tabular Spar from Bucks County, Pennsylvania, with a Notice of Various Minerals found in the same Locality." During the same year he contributed to the *Journal of the Academy of Natural Sciences*, Philadelphia, a "Description of a New Species of Ostrea Convexa of Say." These papers were followed in rapid succession by many other scientific communications, and the journal of the Academy continued to be enriched by his labors until within a short period of his death. There were not less than forty of these contributions, besides others published in the "Transactions of the American Philosophical Society" and the *American Journal of Science and Arts*, edited by Professor Silliman. These articles, by their varied range, exhibited great versatility of talent, treating as they did upon subjects connected with anatomy, ethnology, archæology, geology, paleontology, zoology, and mineralogy. His celebrated monograph on the "Cretaceous Group of the United States" was received, at the time of its publication, with great favor by the most eminent geologists of Europe. In 1834 he contributed to medical literature an important work on "Illustrations of Pulmonary Consumption: its Anatomical Characters, Causes, Symptoms, and Treatment." He early began to make his celebrated collection of crania, and up to 1840 had, with great labor and cost, succeeded in collecting no less than fourteen hundred and sixty eight crania. In 1839 he gave to the world his "Crania Americana," and in 1844 his "Crania Egyptiaca," both of which were very favorably received. In 1849 he published a "System of Human Anatomy." For some years, and at the time of his death, he was President of the Academy of Natural Sciences, of Philadelphia.

He died on May 15, 1851. He was referred to as the "Humboldt of America." In the annals of science his name will always be associated with that of Blumenbach, the founder of human craniology. To this study he gave a powerful impetus by demonstrating the precise method in accordance with which it should be pursued, and by indicating its capability of throwing light upon the origin and affiliations of the various races of men.

The late Dr. Charles D. Meigs, in a biographical sketch written for the Academy of Natural Sciences, says, "Doctor Morton was a man above the ordinary stature; his face was oval, and always pale; his eyes a clear bluish-gray; his hair light. As a man, he was modest in his demeanor, of no arrogant pretensions, and of forgiving temper; charitable and respectful to others, yet never forgetful of self-respect. That he was a religious man I know from many opportunities had with him, and from his life and conversation. He was always in earnest, and always to be depended upon. Few men are to be found more free from faults, and few of greater probity, or of more liberal sentiments, or purer designs and aspirations. Doubtless he had faults, but they were not obvious, and I never discovered them in an acquaintance of near thirty years with him."

An interesting and important feature in the social life of Dr. Morton was the Sunday evening reception held for many years at his home, for the purpose of bringing together his scientific friends. Among those frequently seen upon these delightful and instructive occasions were the Audubons, father and son; Silliman the elder; George Combe, of Edinburgh; Sir Charles Lyell, William Maclure, Prince Charles Bonaparte, the ornithologist; Louis Agassiz, Prince de Wied, Haldeman, Joseph Leidy, and others too numerous to mention.

Dr. Morton's correspondence with scientists at home and abroad was believed to be larger then that of any other one in this country. He was in communication with Baron George Cuvier, Alexander Humboldt, Bunsen, Lepsius, and a host of other distinguished men of letters and science.

The following translation of a letter, acknowledging the receipt of a copy of "Crania Americana," shows the kindly feeling which existed between Dr. Morton and the distinguished author of "Cosmos":

"SIR,—The close bonds of interest and affection that have for the past half-century connected me with the hemisphere in which you reside, and of which I flatter myself that I am a citizen, have added to the impressions made upon me by the receipt, almost at the same moment, of your great work on Philosophical Physiology, and the admirable History of the Conquest of Mexico by Mr. Wm. Prescott. Works of this class, which extend by very different means the sphere of our knowledge, serve to add to the glory of one's country. I cannot sufficiently express my deep gratitude to you.

"At my advanced age, I am peculiarly gratified by the interest still preserved for me beyond the great Atlantic valley over which a bridge has, as it were, been thrown by the power of steam.

"The craniological treasures which you have been so fortunate as to unite in your collection, have in you found a worthy interpreter. Your work is equally remarkable for the profundity of its anatomical views, the numerical detail of the relations of organic conformation, the absence of those poetical reveries which are as the myths of modern physiology, and the generalizations with which your Introductory Essay abounds.

"Being at present occupied in the preparation of the most important of my works, which will be published under the imprudent title of *Cosmos*, I shall know how to profit by so many excellent views upon the distribution of the races of mankind that are scattered throughout your beautiful volume. One cannot, indeed, but be surprised to see in it such evidences of artistic perfection, and that you could produce a work that is a fitting rival of whatever most beautiful has been produced either in France or in England. I pray you to accept the renewed expression of the high consideration with which I have the honor to be, sir, your obedient, humble servant,

"ALEXANDER HUMBOLDT.

"BERLIN, 17th January, 1844."

Dr. Morton was elected an honorary member of very many scientific societies in various parts of the United States, in Europe, and in the East, among which are the following:

The Academy of Natural Sciences, of Philadelphia.
The Philadelphia Medical Society.
The College of Physicians, of Philadelphia.
The American Philosophical Society.
The American Medical Association.
The Massachusetts Medical Society.
The Western Academy of Natural Sciences, at St. Louis.
The Georgia Historical Society.
The American Oriental Society, at Boston.
The American Ethnological Society, at New York.
The Medical Society of Sweden.

The Royal Society of Northern Antiquaries, at Copenhagen.

The Academy of Sciences, Letters, and Arts, de Zelanti di Acireale.

The Imperial Society of Naturalists, of Moscow.

The Medical Society of Edinburgh.

The Senckenburg Natural History Society, of Frankfort-on-the-Main.

BRIGADIER-GENERAL JAMES ST. CLAIR MORTON.

Brigadier-General James St. Clair Morton, of the Engineer Corps of the United States army, son of Dr. Samuel G. Morton, was born September 24, 1829, in the city of Philadelphia. He was appointed a cadet at West Point Military Academy by Hon. Joseph R. Ingersoll, of Philadelphia, member of Congress, where he graduated with much honor in 1851. His first military duty was performed at Charleston, South Carolina, in 1851–52, as assistant engineer in the completion of the harbor fortifications. Major Morton was selected by the Navy Department to make an exploration of the Chiriqui country, South America, to test the practicability of an interoceanic railroad route across the Isthmus at a point midway between the present Panama and Nicaragua routes. On his return to Washington he was placed in charge of the entire work of the Washington aqueduct.

In 1861 he was sent to the Gulf of Mexico for the purpose of putting the fortifications of the Dry Tortugas in a state of defence. In May, 1862, he reported for duty to General Halleck, and was assigned as chief engineer of the Army of the Ohio, under General Buell. When General Buell's troops marched to Kentucky he was ordered to remain at Nashville, where, in conjunction with Generals Negley and Palmer, he superintended the defences of the city. When the Army of the Cumberland was given in charge of General Rosecrans, he was placed in command of the pioneer brigade. At the battle of Stone River, and on subsequent occasions, he proved that he was as brave as he was skilful.

Major Morton was made first lieutenant July 1, 1856, and on the 6th of August, 1861, was promoted to captain. He was nominated brigadier-general of volunteers, to date from November 29, 1862, and was chief engineer to General Rosecrans until October 10, 1863.

He was then ordered to report to General Burnside as chief engineer of the Ninth Corps, with the rank of major.

He was killed in an assault at Petersburg, June 17, 1864.

The following despatch was sent by the Secretary of War, announcing General Morton's death:

"WASHINGTON, D.C., June 19, 1864.

"To DR. THOMAS G. MORTON.

"I have sent to General Grant's head-quarters an order to have the body of Major Morton embalmed and sent to your address at Philadelphia.

"The Department has received no particulars, but the simple announcement that he was killed in an assault upon the enemy's works at Petersburg. He was esteemed in the Department as a brave and gallant officer, and his loss is deeply regretted. Any particulars that may be received will be transmitted to you.

"Signed, E. M. STANTON."

HONORABLE MENTION OF GENERAL JAMES ST. CLAIR MORTON.

Graduating second at the United States Military Academy in 1851, in a class of over forty members, and recommended to the President for promotion in the Engineers and all other arms of the service. (Recorded on page 42 Miscellaneous Book United States Military Academy.)

By the Board of Visitors at the United States Military Academy in 1857, in their report to the Secretary of War, as author of a paper "containing excellent common-sense views" relating to instruction. Said paper was, in accordance with the request of the Board, appended to the Secretary of War's report for 1857–58, and printed with it.

The Light-House Board, in their annual report for 1858 to the Secretary of the Treasury, mention the works of renovation and repair (and the general duties of the light-house establishment) as having been carried on with "energy and ability" in Lieutenant Morton's district.

By the Secretary of War, in his annual report to Congress for 1858, as having submitted a "practical and judicious plan" for certain defensive works, the memoir explanatory of which was "recommended to the consideration of Congress," and printed with the report. (Thirty-fifth Congress, Second Session, Executive Document 2; twelfth appended document.)

By the Secretary of War, in report of 1859, as the author of a memoir on American fortifications "worthy of the notice" of Congress. This memoir was printed with said report in executive documents: Senate Executive Document 2, Thirty-sixth Congress, Second Session; appended document to the Secretary of War's report.

By the chief of the Chiriqui Commission to the Secretary of the Navy, as having conducted his exploration in Central America with "a decision and energy worthy of high praise." (Message of the President to Congress, dated January 22, 1861, Executive Document 41, Thirty-sixth Congress, Second Session.)

By the commander of the United States bark J. C. Chambers to the Secretary of the Navy, for aid rendered his vessel by Lieutenant Morton, who sailed to her on a stormy night in a schooner with a large party of laborers and an extempore outfit of wreckers' material, and got her off a dangerous reef. For this Lieutenant Morton received the thanks of the Navy Department, as follows:

"NAVY DEPARTMENT, March 24, 1862.

"SIR,—The Department desires to express its thanks for your prompt assistance in rescuing from her perilous situation the United States armed bark J. C. Chambers, which vessel had grounded on the night of the 14th ultimo, near South-West Key.

"Signed, GIDEON WELLES."

By Brigadier-General J. S. Negley, who commanded Nashville during its blockade in 1862, when Lieutenant Morton had sole charge of the fortifications of the place, to Major Siddell, Acting Assistant Adjutant-General on General Buell's staff, as follows, viz.:

". . . Whatever success has attended my administration in Nashville, much is due to your intelligent counsels and to the *eminent ability*, *masterly skill*, and *untiring energy* of Captains Morton and Townsend, with the friendly co-operation of the other gentlemen." (General Negley's letter, dated Nashville, November 10, 1862.)

By the commander of the Fourteenth Army Corps to the Secretary of War, in a telegraphic despatch, for services at the battle of Stone River, as follows:

"January 3, while reconnoitring the ground occupied by this division, which had no artillery, I saw a heavy force advancing in line of battle, three lines deep. They drove our little division before them after a sharp contest, in which we lost seventy or eighty killed and three hundred and seventy-five wounded; but the enemy was repulsed by Negley's division and the remaining troops of the left wing, headed by Morton's Pioneer Brigade," etc.

Captain Morton was recommended, also by telegraph, by the said commander, for brigadier-general, and was promised it by telegraph by President Lincoln and the Secretary of War, for his services on this occasion. And in the official report of the battle by General Rosecrans is the following mention, viz.:

"Among the lesser commands which deserve special mention for distinguished services in the battle is the Pioneer Corps, a body of seventeen hundred men, composed of details from the companies of each infantry regiment, organized and instructed by Captain J. St. C. Morton, Corps of Engineers, chief engineer of this army, which marched as an infantry brigade with the left wing, made bridges at Stewart's Creek, prepared and guarded the ford at Stone River on the nights of the 29th and 30th, supported Stokes's battery, and fought with valor and determination on the 31st, holding its position until relieved; on the morning of the 2d advancing with the greatest promptitude and gallantry to support Van Cleve's division against the attack on our left on the evening of the same day; constructing a bridge and batteries between that time and Saturday evening; and the efficiency and *esprit de corps* suddenly developed in this command, its gallant behavior in action, the eminent service it is continually rendering the army, entitle both officers and men to special public notice and thanks, while they reflect the highest credit on the distinguished ability and capacity of Captain Morton, who will do honor to his promotion to a brigadier-general, which the President has promised him." (Nominated brigadier-general by President Lincoln and confirmed by the Senate.)

By the commander of the Army of the Cumberland, in his official report of the battle of Chickamauga, in which General Morton was wounded, as having performed his duty "with ability and to his [General Rosecrans's] entire satisfaction."

By the same, in *General Orders*, dated Chattanooga, Tennessee, October 10, 1863, General Order No. 231, as follows, viz.:

". . . The General Commanding thanks Brigadier-General J. St. C. Morton for the zeal and energy he has always displayed in the discharge of the duties of Chief Engineer." . . .

Exclusive of the essays referred to above, Captain Morton was the author of a "Memoir on Fortifications," printed by order of the War Department; a "Memoir of the Life and Services of Major Sanders, of the Engineer Corps, dedicated to the Officers of the Corps;" a "Report on the Water Supply of Certain Cities of the United States;" a "Report on the Practicability of an Interoceanic Railroad on the Isthmus of Chiriqui" (printed Executive Document 41, Thirty-sixth Congress, Second Session); and numerous minor pieces. He designed the fortifications of Murfreesboro' and of Nashville, known as Fortress Rosecrans, Fort Negley, Fort Houston, Fort Andrew Johnson, Fort Morton, etc., and many other important civil and military works, including a large part of the defences of Chattanooga, particularly the intrenched lines which sheltered our army so completely on their retreat thither from Chickamauga.

He several times received the commendation of the chief of the Engineer Corps, particularly for a plan of the citadel and other fortifications of Quebec, prepared from a personal survey made by Captain Morton in 1855 (under the difficulties which always attend the acquisition of such knowledge), aided in regard to certain details by a brother officer; and, secondly, for continuing, on his own responsibility, in the absence of instructions from superior authority, to push with the utmost despatch the work of construction necessary to place Fort Jefferson (commanding the harbor of the Tortugas) in a defensive condition, at the time of the "Mason and Slidell" difficulty with England. At that time all funds available for the said operations were exhausted, and all the liabilities incurred, amounting to over sixty thousand dollars, were at Captain Morton's own risk.

A distinguished officer in the most distinguished corps of the

INDEX.

Ck

S.

www.ingramcontent.com/pod-product-compliance
Lightning Source LLC
Chambersburg PA
CBHW031117020726
47495CB00007B/2238